P9-BZG-709

continued . . .

A Deal to Die For

"A great cozy with a wonderful balance of humor, tension, and romance. Maggie and the rest of the Good Buy Girls create a wonderful core group of characters who are each interesting in their own way . . . A great book."
—Fresh Fiction

"With her wry humor, Maggie and her friends return to entertain the reader with their shopping strategies, unwavering friendship, and their deductive investigating skills . . . Josie Belle conducted some deft strategies of her own when she shaped this series into being."   —Once Upon a Romance

"The mystery was complex and the secrets are revealed in such a way that keeps the reader guessing right up to the very special moment where everything falls into place."
—Escape with Dollycas Into a Good Book

"An interesting and fun cozy mystery populated by a host of quirky and enjoyable characters."
—Curling Up by the Fire

"I absolutely couldn't put this book down . . . The mystery will definitely keep you guessing 'til the end, and the characters will have you coming back for more!"
—A Prairie Girl Reads

50% off Murder

"If you love to shop 'til you drop, watch out for Josie Belle's first entry in a new mystery series—because murder's no bargain."
—Leann Sweeney, *New York Times* bestselling author of *The Cat, the Sneak and the Secret*

"An engaging mystery full of humor, a layered plot, and even a little romance."

—Amy Alessio, author of the Alana O'Neill Mysteries

"*50% off Murder* is a great deal: there's mystery, romance, and humor wrapped up in one entertaining package. As a bonus, there's no extra charge for those laugh-out-loud moments. I look forward to many more adventures from Maggie and her friends . . . Meanwhile, bring on those money-saving tips!"

—Mary Jane Maffini, author of the Charlotte Adams Mysteries

"A fun, well-plotted mystery with the added bonus of some money-saving tips." —The Mystery Reader

"Best friends, bargain hunting, and murder! This new cozy mystery series has great promise and I'm looking forward to seeing what the bargain-hunting babes of St. Stanley will be up to next." —Novel Reflections

"Good, solid writing, well-formed characters, an enjoyable premise, a possible romance in the making, and a mystery that slowly unfolds its secrets. A bargain read for sure!"

—Once Upon a Romance

"What an enjoyable read! I loved the spunky Maggie."

—TwoLips Reviews

"The Good Buy Girls love a good deal—and a good murder . . . The debut of an all-new mystery series—and it's worth every penny." —I Dream Books

continued . . .

All Sales Final

Josie Belle

BERKLEY PRIME CRIME, NEW YORK

BERKLEY PRIME CRIME

An imprint of Penguin Random House LLC
375 Hudson Street, New York, New York 10014

ALL SALES FINAL

A Berkley Prime Crime Book / published by arrangement with the author

ISBN: 978-0-425-27137-7

PUBLISHING HISTORY
Berkley Prime Crime mass-market edition / September 2015

PRINTED IN THE UNITED STATES OF AMERICA

10 9 8 7 6 5 4 3 2 1

Cover illustration by Mary Ann Lasher.
Cover design by Sarah Oberrender.
Interior text design by Laura K. Corless.

Penguin
Random
House

This book is dedicated to all of the readers who have enjoyed the zany adventures of the Good Buy Girls as much as I have enjoyed writing them. Thank you!

Chapter 1

"Why can't I just wear a dress I already own?" Maggie asked. She knew her voice had reached a whiney pitch but she didn't care enough to try and make it less grating. Her feet hurt, her back ached and she was pretty sure she'd pulled a muscle in her butt, trying to wriggle into the last dress Ginger had foisted upon her.

"Maggie Gerber, you are not walking down the aisle to Sam Collins in a dress you already own," Ginger Lancaster said. A fine sheen of sweat coated her dark complexion; clearly Maggie wasn't the only one exerting herself in this quest for the perfect bridal gown.

Maggie had refused to wear white. She was in her forties. She'd already been married and had a grown daughter, and wearing white just seemed too ingénue to her. Unfortunately, her auburn hair and pale freckled skin ruled out a lot of color options.

Then there was the issue that Maggie was a founder of a self-named group of bargain hunters called the Good Buy Girls, who pretty much lived for savings and thrift. She simply could not spend a fortune on a dress she was going to wear for just one day. It went against the code.

If it had been left up to Maggie, she would have worn the gown she had worn to the Madison Ball in December, but her friends wouldn't hear of it.

"Ginger's right. Besides your favorite was a long-sleeved, high-necked dress that would be suffocating to wear in June," Joanne Claramotta said. She glanced up from the stroller that carried her baby girl Patience, or as her daddy liked to call her, Patty Cake.

"And the olive color, while gorgeous in December, is a bit somber for a June wedding," Claire Freemont chimed in. "Not to mention the back."

"What back?" Ginger asked and they all broke out laughing. "Oh yeah, Pastor Shields would keel over dead if he got a gander at all that skin in his house of worship."

Maggie heaved a sigh. "I could wear a veil that would cover the open back."

"No. Just no," Ginger said and shook her head at her.

"Fine," Maggie said. "But I look like Tinker Bell in this thing so it's a no, too."

"Oh, I think it's cute," Joanne said.

Maggie glanced at her friend. Clearly, she was suffering from some postpartum fashion impairment. The bodice of the dress Maggie currently had on was sparkly silver and the skirt looked like a puffy tutu in layers of pink and purple tulle. She wouldn't have been caught dead in this dress, and she was pretty sure Ginger had only made her put it on to amuse herself. One glance at Ginger's face, which was contorted from trying not to laugh, confirmed it.

"You're right," Maggie said. She spun a sloppy pirouette in the dressing room's three-way mirror. "It is cute. You know, I think I'll take it."

"Gah! What?" Ginger squawked.

"Aha!" Maggie pointed at her. "You were pranking me with this dress."

"Maybe, a little," Ginger said. She looked down. "Claire bet me five bucks I couldn't get you to try it on."

"Ah," Maggie gasped. "Claire!"

"What?" Claire asked. She pushed her black glasses up on her nose. "I'm the one who's out five bucks. I don't know why you're upset. Besides we've been at this for five hours. We've hit every bridal store within a fifty mile radius of St. Stanley. Honestly, how can we not have found you a reasonably priced but still amazing dress yet?"

"I don't know," Maggie said. "But this poufy sparkly thing is giving me a headache." She glanced at the skin on her chest. "And possibly a rash."

"Here, let's get you out of it," Ginger said and she spun Maggie around and unzipped her.

Maggie sucked in a deep gulp of air and ducked behind the curtain to get dressed. When she returned with the offending dress and three other rejects on her arm, she handed them to the waiting saleslady and signaled to the girls that it was time to go.

As they passed a bride and her mother, Maggie felt a pang in her chest. She missed her daughter, Laura, who was doing an internship in New York City this summer. Oh, she'd be in Virginia to stand up for Maggie at the wedding, and Maggie knew that Laura loved Sam and was happy for them, but her baby girl would be finishing college soon and was starting her own life. It was one of the many changes Maggie had been trying to adjust to over the past few months.

"Don't worry," Ginger said as she draped her arm over Maggie's shoulder. "It's only May; we have almost a month to find your perfect dress."

Maggie returned her friend's half hug. She didn't have the heart to tell her that it wasn't just the dress that had her fretting. She and Sam had decided to start their new life in a new house, a place that they owned together, which would be a new beginning for both of them. While she was thrilled by the idea of a fresh start, leaving her home of more than twenty years was harder than she had thought it would be.

"I know you're right," she said. She didn't want to burden her friends with all of her thoughts. "No worries."

Joanne had been the designated driver since she needed Patience's car seat. They all piled into her SUV with Ginger sitting next to Patience so she could coo at the baby while they drove. As the mother of four teen boys, Ginger could not get enough of the precious baby girl.

"If not ivory or white, then what color do you want to wear to your wedding?" Claire asked from the front passenger seat. "I can research customs for second weddings for you at the library. Maybe there is something mystical about wearing red or purple."

Claire glanced over her seat back at Maggie. With her blond bob and rectangular black glasses, Claire looked just like the librarian that she was. She was always the one to answer a conundrum with research and Maggie valued her for it.

"That might give us some interesting ideas," Joanne said. "Maybe yellow could be your go-to color."

She tossed her long brown braid over her shoulder and met Maggie's gaze in the rearview mirror, then her eyes darted to the baby just to be sure her girl was fine. It had taken Joanne and her husband, Michael, a long time to conceive and Maggie frequently caught her friend staring at her baby girl in wonder. She understood the feeling well.

"Yellow?" Maggie asked. "I don't know if that color is always kind to redheads."

"Just be thankful that your only issue is finding a dress. I've been reading up on international wedding customs and there are some doozies," Claire said. "In Fiji, the groom must present his prospective father-in-law with a whale tooth. Biggest mammal going and it lives under water, how's that for proving your love?"

"Sam is getting off easy," Ginger said.

"There is also a tribal custom in northern Borneo where the newly married couples are required to be confined to their house while not going to the bathroom for three days and nights," Claire said. "Now that's commitment."

"Suddenly, finding an appropriate dress does not seem as much of a challenge as it did a few minutes ago," Maggie said. She grinned at her friend. "Thank you, Claire."

"You're quite welcome," Claire said.

"How do you know all of these things?" Ginger asked. "It mystifies."

"We information scientists are full of useful facts," Claire said. "I know a few more unusual customs."

"No, no, I think we're good." Ginger held up one hand. "I don't want to ruin my lunch."

"Can you drop me off at the station, Joanne?" Maggie said. "Sam and I have an appointment with Marcy Hayes."

"No problem, what property are you looking at today?" Joanne asked.

Maggie glanced at her friends. She wondered how they were going to take the news. She could still hear her mother's gasp of horror from when she'd spoken to her on the phone last night. Well, there wasn't any way to sugarcoat it.

"The Dixon place," she said.

The rest of the the Good Buy Girls looked at her with wide eyes. They wore matching expressions of disbelief and not the sort that meant they'd found a Louis Vuitton handbag in perfect condition at 75% off. Instead, they looked as though they'd found an imitation Coach bag for sale but still priced at more than its retail value.

"I know what you're going to say," Maggie said. "My mother let me have it with both barrels last night."

"That the place has been empty for over five years and there's probably a family of skunks living in it," Ginger said. Obviously, there was no warning her off of the subject.

"There are no varmints living in it," Maggie said. "At least, I don't think so."

"Well how about the fact that the yard is so overgrown it's begun to swallow up the neighborhood pets that stray too close to the picket fence, which is falling down," Claire said.

"A landscaper was over there last week, making everything nice and tidy again," Maggie said. "As far as I know, they found no carcasses of missing pets."

Joanne didn't say anything and Maggie met her gaze in the rearview mirror. Her friend looked worried.

"What is it, Joanne?" Maggie asked. "You may as well say your piece, too."

"Nothing," she said with a forced smile.

"You're a terrible liar, Joanne," Ginger said. "Go ahead and say it. We're all thinking it."

"I heard it's haunted," Joanne said. She clamped her lips together quickly as if by closing her mouth she could disassociate herself from her own words.

"That's just a rumor," Maggie said. "Of course people think it's haunted. It's been in the Dixon family for generations with its last residents being two spinster sisters. I think that means it has a rich family history. I don't think it means it's haunted."

They were all quiet as Joanne navigated the winding road back to town.

"Maybe," Ginger said. "But are you willing to risk it?"

Chapter 2

Sam Collins was waiting outside the station when Joanne pulled up to let Maggie out. As always, Maggie's heart beat a little faster at the sight of him. His brown hair was peppered with gray, and his bright blue eyes had crinkles in the corners, but he was still as big and strong as he had been when he was eighteen and Maggie was seventeen and they'd fallen in love the first time around.

More than twenty years and a lot of living had kept them apart but Sam had moved back to St. Stanley after retiring from the Richmond PD. He was sheriff for their small town and as circumstances had thrown them together over the past year and then some, he and Maggie had discovered they had unfinished business. Now they were getting married. It boggled.

As Maggie climbed out of the car, Ginger quickly grabbed her and held her still. Then she took off the cross she always wore around her neck and pressed it into Maggie's hand.

"Just in case," Ginger said.

Maggie rolled her eyes but draped the necklace over her head to hang around her neck just to make her best friend since preschool happy.

"Text us," Claire said. "ASAP."

"Yes, anytime," Joanne added. "You know I'm up all night."

"It'll be fine," Maggie said. "But yes, I promise I'll check in."

She waved as the van pulled away. Sam joined her at the curb and gave her a quick hug.

"What's up with the thrifty three?" he asked.

"Ghosts," she said.

Sam frowned at her. "Whose?"

"Ours. They are concerned that we are looking at a haunted house," Maggie said.

"The Dixon house?" he asked. "Nah, it just needs a little love, or possibly a wrecking ball."

Maggie laughed. "I like your flexibility. Let's not keep Marcy waiting. I swear she almost swooned when I told her we would look at it."

"Did you tell her we were bringing a third opinion?" Sam asked.

"No, I thought I'd leave that to you," Maggie said.

Sam smiled. He led Maggie to the car and opened the door. Curled up on the passenger seat waiting for them was Marshall Dillon, Sam's cat, who was now their shared cat. A gray tabby with a distinctive stripe in the shape of an *M* on his forehead, he liked to ride around in Sam's squad car and spent most of his days in the station. Maggie was pretty sure Sam would have deputized him if he could.

Maggie scooped Marshall Dillon up and then sat down, replacing him on her lap. Sam took the driver's seat and they buckled up and headed over to the historic part of town.

The Dixon house was one of the oldest houses in St. Stanley. It wasn't as big as some of the mansions on the street but it was a beautiful two-story Victorian with a wraparound porch and arch-shaped windows on the upper level. Maggie had always admired it and she had even occasionally daydreamed about having a place like this of her very own.

The grass was freshly mowed and the bushes had been trimmed back, but it still had an untamed air about it. The house badly needed a coat of fresh paint and the windows longed for some elbow grease but the bones were all there. Like any aging beauty, with a little upkeep, Maggie felt certain it would be spectacular again.

Sam pulled up in front of the house. Maggie carried Marshall Dillon to the front porch where Marcy Hayes was waiting.

Marcy was a very earnest woman, a single mom with two teenagers. She worked seven days a week doing

listings, showings and open houses, all in an effort to provide since her husband ran off with a woman half his
age and was selfish enough to clean out their bank
account on his way out of town.

Maggie glanced at Sam as they climbed the steps to
the porch. He didn't seem the type to have a midlife crisis
but then she was pretty sure Marcy would have said the
same thing about her husband. She glanced at the house.
If Sam did leave her, would she want to live here alone?

Marshall Dillon hissed which made Maggie jump and
she let him go. He leapt down onto the porch with the
scruff of his neck in an agitated ruff and his tail fluffed.

"Well, hello there, little fella."

Marcy knelt down and wiggled her fingers at Marshall
Dillon then made kissy noises. Maggie did not think Marshall Dillon was going to go for this in the least but he
lowered his head and plowed toward Marcy, not stopping
until she was scratching him under the chin and he was
purring. His fur slowly lowered from its full alert state.

"What do you suppose that was about?" Maggie
asked Sam.

"Maybe he smelled another cat in the area. The place
has been empty for a while. It could be we have some feral
cats living under the porch."

Maggie looked at him. "I like the way you've already
mentally moved in."

"Noticed that, huh?" he asked.

Marcy rose to her feet and Marshall Dillon twined
around her ankle.

"He is just precious," she said. "I think he'd really love

having such a big house to play in, and maybe you could even get him a friend."

"We were thinking about a dog," Sam said.

"Oh, the backyard is just perfect for a dog," Marcy said. "So much room to run and play."

Maggie pressed her lips together. She had a feeling they could say they were going to breed elephants and Marcy would find a way to make the house the perfect location for them.

"Let's go inside and I'll give you the room-by-room tour," she said.

Sam gestured for Maggie to follow Marcy first. She had a feeling Marcy wasn't going to have to work too hard to sell Sam on the place. As for her, this was probably the biggest change she'd made in her life since she quit her job working for Dr. Franklin, bought her own business and started dating Sam.

Okay, now that she considered it that was a lot of change in the past few years, and all since Sam came back to town. Maybe buying a house together would be the final upheaval for a while. She tried not to think about how leaving her home of so many years was going to feel.

She stepped into the foyer with Marshall Dillon scampering ahead. There was no furniture in the house. Wainscoting was the only decoration on the walls. It looked prim and proper but homey, too. The floors were hardwood and polished to a high gloss.

Maggie's footsteps echoed in the empty rooms, and then Sam's joined hers and it didn't sound so lonely anymore.

"This is the front parlor," Marcy said. "It could be turned into a library, however, and the fireplace is original but was converted to gas about ten years ago."

Maggie crossed to the fireplace. The mantel shelf looked good and strong, the perfect place to put all of the pictures of their loved ones. Sam's hand slid into hers and he laced her fingers with his.

"We could put a loveseat right here," he said. "And read in front of the fire on cold winter evenings."

"Oh, that sounds nice," Maggie said.

"Through here is the formal dining room," Marcy called as she disappeared through a door on the far side of the room.

It was a large space with a big bay window that over-looked the side yard. Maggie could see her own dining room table in here. It would look amazing when set with her grandmother's china for the holidays.

"The kitchen is in here," Marcy called, still trotting on ahead. Maggie wondered if Marcy was moving at such a fast pace because she had another appointment or because she didn't want them to linger in the house. Hmm.

Marcy didn't sound as peppy as she had before and Maggie got the feeling Marcy was hoping to finish up quickly with something distasteful. As soon as Maggie and Sam stepped into the kitchen, Maggie knew what Marcy had been dreading.

The kitchen was sparkling clean, but it was also locked somewhere in the year 1956 with gray steel cabinets, aqua tile countertops and even a matching aqua refrigerator.

Maggie ran her hand over the counter. It was in perfect condition with no chips or cracks, hard to believe for something that was easily sixty years old. The range was an old O'Keefe and Merritt gas and was equally spotless.

"Does it work?" she asked Marcy.

"Oh yes," Marcy said. "There were some renters here a few years back. They said everything was in tip-top shape. I know it isn't state-of-the-art."

"No, it's more like art, period," Maggie said. "Oh, I love vintage kitchens."

Sam grinned.

"You knew it was all vintage, didn't you?" she asked.

He nodded. "I'd heard the kitchen was remodeled in the fifties and hadn't been touched since. I figured you'd dig it."

Marcy's eyes went wide. "You like it as it is?"

"Like it?" Maggie asked. "I love it. I specialize in retro at the shop. I think I even have a copper canister from the fifties that would look amazing over there."

"Well, isn't this perfect?" Marcy spread her arms wide. She was beaming.

"Yes, it is actually," Maggie said. Each room was better than the last and she was really beginning to see Sam and her making their life together here.

The master bedroom and bath had been modernized and updated. A big bay window with a love seat looked out over the two acre backyard. There was a walk-in closet that was as big as Maggie's bedroom now, and the large master bath had another bay window and a Jacuzzi.

There were several more bedrooms and a sitting room

upstairs and Maggie and Sam haggled over which would be their home office and which would be guest bedrooms. Maggie didn't really care and only put up a bit of resistance just to keep Sam on his toes.

She had been alone for a very long time. The thought of sharing the three Bs—bed, bathroom and bills—with someone again made her feel just a bit light-headed. She wasn't used to making compromises; she was used to making all the decisions and doing all the heavy lifting. What would it be like to lighten the load? She could barely fathom it.

Marcy's cell phone rang and she glanced at it. "I'm sorry. I have to take this. You two go ahead and wander about, and I'll meet you on the porch when you're done."

Sam and Maggie poked their heads in the attic. It was dry and dusty with a few cobwebs and a bit of a draft but there was no sign of any critters of the furry or the insect sort. They also checked out the basement which, aside from creaky wooden stairs, was dark and dank but dry and free of mold.

They examined the overgrown garden just outside the kitchen window. Maggie could just picture replanting it with an herb garden. She'd always wanted to plant parsley, sage, rosemary and thyme, well, just because. And she wanted to plant tomatoes since there was nothing like fresh tomatoes in summer.

Sam was thrilled to discover that the toolshed at the back end of the property was big enough for a ride-on mower. Maggie noticed that the woods beyond the lawn looked friendly and cheerful, the sort of place deer and bunnies would roam, as opposed to being cold and creepy and full of monsters.

At least Maggie imagined it that way, but maybe that was because she was falling in love with the house as quickly as she'd fallen in love with Sam. She knew from experience that when something was right, you could feel it all the way down in your bones. This house felt right. As they strode across the lawn, Sam put his arm around her shoulders and pulled her close.

He leaned down and kissed her temple as they both examined the back of the house. It did need paint and some more landscaping. But the wraparound porch was just begging for a swing and Maggie could see herself sitting on it with Sam as they sipped iced tea and watched Marshall Dillon chase butterflies.

"What do you think of it, darling? Do you think we could make a life here together?" Sam asked.

Maggie noted that his voice was carefully neutral as if he didn't want to influence her decision in any way.

"I think . . ." Maggie began but she was interrupted by the loudest screeching meow she had ever heard. It made her heart clutch and the hair rise up on the back of her neck.

"Marshall Dillon!" Maggie and Sam cried together, and they ran toward the house.

Chapter 3

They banged through the back door and into the house.

"Marshall Dillon!" Maggie called.

"MD, where are you, buddy?" Sam called.

He made a soft clucking noise and they both paused to listen for the sound of Marshall Dillon's feet coming toward them or for another howl. There was nothing but oppressive silence.

"Where is he?" Maggie whispered.

"Don't worry," Sam said. "He has to be here somewhere and we'll find him. He's a cat, a particularly curious one."

"You're right. Should we separate?"

Before Maggie could answer the yowl began again and they both started.

"Basement," Sam said. He strode toward the basement door in the hallway.

"We must have shut him in down there," Maggie said with a wince.

Sam yanked the door open and they glanced at the top step. There was no sign of Marshall Dillon. Sam went to take a step into the basement and a ball of fur flew past him and out the door.

Maggie and Sam both jumped back. Sam closed the door and they followed the gray tabby down the hall and into the front room where he scurried into a corner with his back up and his teeth bared.

"Hey, buddy." Sam crouched down. "It's okay. You're all right."

Maggie knelt beside Sam and wiggled her fingers. Marshall Dillon hunkered low and crept forward until he was under Sam's hand. Sam gently rubbed his head and the back of his neck until his fur went down. Then he picked Marshall Dillon up and cradled him close.

Maggie checked all of the kitty's limbs, looking for bites, scratches, missing fur or sore spots but Marshall Dillon looked fine. He even purred and pushed his head against Sam's chest.

"He seems okay," Maggie said.

"Maybe he just scared himself," Sam said.

"Well, it is a deep, dark basement," Maggie said. "Poor guy, maybe he thought we left him."

Sam lifted the kitty until they were nose to nose. "Never gonna happen, buddy."

Marshall Dillon gently batted Sam's nose and Maggie

could swear the cat smiled. She felt a bone-deep chill pass over her skin, and she shivered. Sam saw it and gave her a half hug.

"Well, should we go tell Marcy what we've decided?" Sam asked.

Maggie glanced around the room. "Yes."

"Is that yes, we should tell her or yes, we'll take it?" Sam asked.

"Both," Maggie said and then glanced at him. "That is, if you want to."

Sam grinned. "Heck, yeah! Well, Maggie O'Brien Gerber, soon to be Maggie O'Brien Gerber Collins, it looks like we have a home."

The light-headedness hit again, but Maggie was sure it was just a rush of joy and not a panic attack. Okay, she was mostly sure and even if it was panic she told herself that it was okay because it was sort of like manic happiness, right?

Marcy was just ending her call as they joined her on the porch. She turned to look at them with wary eyes. Maggie assumed she was being cautious and not wanting to get her hopes up about a sale.

Maggie knew the feeling. In her consignment shop, Maggie frequently had people come in and eyeball an expensive dress or piece of furniture and it was agony when they kept coming back to look but wouldn't commit to making the purchase. She didn't want to do that to Marcy.

"We'll take it," Maggie said.

Marcy just stared at them as if she was waiting for the

punch line, which was amusing because Marcy wasn't the kind of gal to joke around, especially about real estate.

Everything about Marcy was a statement in efficiency. She wore her brown hair in a fashionable bob. Her suit was flattering: not too boxy and not too sexy but just right. Her pumps were sensibly thick heeled and made for walking around houses for hours and hours while still being stylish.

She wasn't one to flirt or tease. She took her listings and her sales very seriously, wanting to sell homes but also to make sure everyone was happy.

Sam and Maggie glanced at each other. Marcy wasn't moving.

"Marcy, did you hear Maggie? We'll take it," Sam said.

"The house?" Marcy clarified.

"Yes, the house, this house," Maggie said. "We would like to buy it."

"You would?" Marcy asked. "Oh, my gracious. You're not teasing me? You mean it."

"Of course we do," Sam said.

"We wouldn't tease you about something like that," Maggie said.

"Oh!" Marcy pressed both of her hands to her mouth as if trying to keep in a whoop of joy. Then she threw her arms wide and hugged both Maggie and Sam with Marshall Dillon squished in the middle. "I can't believe it. I've finally sold the Dixon house after five long years. This is amazing. I just know you're going to be so happy here."

As she started to cry, Maggie met Sam's gaze over

Marcy's head and she grinned. Reducing your Realtor to happy tears of joy had to be a good sign, right?

"Maggie, you need to make a decision about the venue for your wedding. Did you get a dress yet? What about flowers? Daffodils are lovely."

Maggie would have said something but since her mother, Lizzie O'Brien, didn't pause for breath it didn't seem her input was warranted.

As her mother continued to grill her about the wedding, Maggie puttered around the house that had been her home since she had said yes to Charlie Gerber more than twenty years before.

It was small and cozy. Just right for a widowed mom and her young daughter, which was why Maggie had never moved. Well, that and the fact that making ends meet had meant living simply and cheaply without a lot of extras. The kitchen was woefully out of date as were the floors, the doors and the baths. In fact, she wondered if her love of vintage came from the fact that her home was still very much in its original state.

As she walked from the living room to the kitchen, she ran a finger over the pencil marks that had charted her daughter's height through the years. She'd have to remember to take a picture of it for posterity's sake. The last mark made was right before Laura left for college in Pennsylvania. How had the years passed so swiftly?

The corner of the living room where their Christmas tree always stood made her chest tighten at the thought that they would never have their beautiful angel smile benevolently down at them from that corner again.

"Maggie, are you listening?"

"Yes, Mom,"

"Good, now about the menu . . ." Lizzie continued with her monologue.

As her mother talked, Maggie walked out to the glassed-in sunroom at the back of her house. Full of comfy wicker furniture, it overlooked her pretty little yard. A warbler was sitting on the edge of the bird bath doing his daily ablutions. She wondered if Sam would be okay with her bringing the bird bath. She knew Marshall Dillon would be happy about it, but she didn't want him to mistake it for an all-he-could-eat bird buffet.

The large dogwood tree was in full flower. It was the same tree Laura had fallen out of when she was seven. She'd only had the wind knocked out of her but Maggie would never forget looking out the window to see her daughter lying still and pale in the yard. She put a hand on her head. She wasn't sure where it was exactly but she knew there was a gray hair attached to that episode.

So many memories and now she was leaving to start a new life with Sam. She had never thought she'd marry again after Charlie. He had been all that was good and kind and losing him had just about killed her. In fact, if it hadn't been for Laura, she wondered if she would ever have pulled out of her grief.

But life had had other plans for her, and Maggie was game. She was ready to start a new life with Sam. She was giddily ecstatic about it, truth be told. She had just never thought she could be so sad and so excited at the same time.

"Your sister wants to talk to you," her mother said, pulling Maggie out of her reverie.

"Oh, okay, love you, Mom," Maggie said.

"Love you, too," her mother said. "And don't worry. Your wedding will be lovely. I'll make sure of it."

"Hey, Magpie," her sister said. She'd been calling Maggie that since they were kids.

"Hey, Sissy," Maggie said. Her sister's real name was Michelle, but Maggie had called her older sibling Sissy from the moment she could talk and the name had stuck.

"Hang on, I'm going out of earshot of Mom," Sissy said.

Maggie heard a door open and close with a creak and slam. Her sister had moved to Florida several years ago, and their mother had joined her shortly after. Maggie loved them dearly and she missed them, but she knew the three of them were as close as they were because of the miles between them. Had Lizzie and Sissy continued to live in St. Stanley, Maggie was quite sure the henpecking and nagging would have driven a wedge between them.

"How are you really?" Sissy asked. "About the wedding and all?"

"I'm good," Maggie said. "With so much going on, I don't really have time to be anything else."

"Are you kidding? You just bought a house," her sister said. "You have to be freaking out."

Maggie had no idea why her sister telling her she *had* to be feeling something made her determined not to feel that way at all. It was like they were still teenagers and she couldn't help her knee-jerk response.

"Well, I'm not," she said. "I'm perfectly fine."

"Liar, liar, pants on fire."

"No, really," Maggie insisted, more determined than ever to prove she was fine. "I couldn't be happier."

"Then why don't you have a venue, a dress, flowers or a caterer for your wedding? Shall I go on?"

Maggie could feel her brain contract. Maybe Florida wasn't far enough away for her mom and sister to live.

"I have plenty of time," Maggie said. "Oh, speaking of, look at that, I have to go. I'm picking up some donations for the shop today. Love you."

"You are not fooling me one little bit, Magpie. We'll talk later. Love you, too," Sissy said just before Maggie ended the call.

Maggie shoved her cell phone into her purse. She hadn't been lying to her sister. She was picking up some donations from the Spring Gardens Assisted Care facility in the heart of town. Her old boss Doc Franklin maintained an office there to make it easier for the seniors who lived there to be able to get to him.

Because she had kept Doc's books for him for over twenty years, Maggie knew the place and the residents well. She was on speed dial for many of them when they wanted to shop at her store or when they wanted to consign some items for a little extra money or to declutter their space.

Today, Maggie had a dual purpose. She was picking

up an Oneida silver set from Rosie Hernandez that her daughters had informed her they didn't want even though it had been in the family for three generations.

Rosie had been so offended she had called Maggie and asked to consign it. She planned to go on a cruise with the money she made from the sale. Since it was a nearly flawless service for twelve, Maggie was pretty sure Rose was going to get her wish.

She locked up her house, trying not to think about the fact that she wouldn't be doing that much longer, and climbed into her Volvo station wagon. She wound her way through her neighborhood and pulled into the gated estate that was Spring Gardens.

Maggie parked in the visitor's lot and crossed the well-manicured green lawn to the entrance of the building. Maggie pushed through the massive door of the remodeled colonial and stopped by the check-in desk.

Barbara York was working the front desk, and she greeted Maggie with a smile.

"Hi, Maggie, you here to pick up Rosie's silver?"

"Yes," Maggie said. "She called me three times yesterday. I think she is eager to sell it and book her cruise."

"Good for her," Barbara said. "If the young ones don't appreciate the finer things then they don't deserve them."

"Agreed," Maggie said. "I also wanted to pop in on Blue Dixon. Is he around?"

"Always," Barbara said. "He's holding court out by the pool."

"Holding court?" Maggie asked.

"You'll see," Barbara said with a small smile.

Maggie met with Rosie and gave her a receipt for her silver, which she then loaded into her car. Once she locked the back of her Volvo, she went back into Spring Gardens, crossed the lobby and went out the far door that led to the pool. There was a water aerobics class going on and several swimmers were doing laps. But off in the far corner under a large canopy was a lounge chair surrounded by deck chairs. Sitting in the lounge chair was a man in a loud Hawaiian shirt and bright orange shorts. Blue Dixon.

He had a thick head of gray hair and a matching neatly trimmed beard. His eyes were full of mischief and he had a booming laugh that echoed out across the water when he paused in his story, clearly amused by his own wit. He gestured with his hands while he talked and the ladies in the chairs sitting around him were listening with rapt attention.

Maggie approached quietly. She had never met Blue Dixon and wanted to get his measure before she engaged him in conversation.

"And then I said to the Duke, 'I'll take that bet, you son of a gun, because I'm the best there's ever been,'" he said.

"Oh, Blue, you didn't," a spry old gal with sparkly earrings and a very well-maintained body said.

"Oh yes, I did," Blue said. "I was in the royal box at Ascot, what else could I do?" he asked.

The ladies all twittered about him and Maggie knew exactly what she was dealing with: a geriatric Lothario of the first order.

"Mr. Dixon?" she asked.

"That's me." Blue's eyes looked her over and he grinned. "What can I do for a pretty little filly such as yourself?"

Maggie gave him her best quelling glance and let her left hand, the one Sam had put a substantial rock on, show. Blue got it right away. He looked chagrined but his smile didn't dim, not even a little.

"You're not my new nurse, are you?"

"Sorry," she said.

"Masseuse?" he asked hopefully.

"Nope," she said. She sat in the lone vacant seat, very aware of the women around them giving her the stink eye. "I'm here to talk to you about your house."

"Business, then," he said. He looked put out but then shrugged. "Ladies, if you'll excuse us, we'll finish up that story later."

"During cocktail hour?" the woman with the sparkly earrings suggested with a wink.

"You know it," he said.

Maggie watched as the ladies left, casting looks of longing over their shoulders as they went.

"You have quite the cushy situation here," Maggie said.

"I can't complain," Blue said. "The one nice thing about getting old is the ratio of women to men is most definitely in a man's favor."

"It's nice to see you sharing yourself so generously," Maggie teased him.

"I do what I can," he said and spread his hands wide. "Since you know my name, may I inquire what yours might be?"

"Oh, I'm sorry, I'm Maggie Gerber. My fiancé Sam Collins and I are buying your house," she said.

She extended her hand and Blue returned her handshake with a solid squeeze and comfortable warmth.

"How about that?" Blue said. "So, you really are going to buy the old place? Marcy has been trying to sell it for almost five years. We've had a few people close to buying it, but they always back out."

"Have they ever told you why?" Maggie asked.

"Usually, it was something about how they didn't like the vibe of the house. Of course this was always after the inspection and after I had fixed whatever they didn't like. You did see the kitchen, right?"

"Oh yes," Maggie said. "I love vintage kitchens. It's perfect."

Blue grinned at her. "Well, maybe you're just destined to be the next resident."

"I hope so," Maggie said. "I just have one question for you."

"What's that?" Blue asked.

"Did any of your relatives ever mention if maybe, well, if the house was haunted?" Maggie asked.

Chapter 4

"'Haunted'?" Blue asked. "As in a ghost?"

"Well, I don't know if I would say a ghost," Maggie hedged. "But maybe a presence."

"A ghost presence?" Blue asked.

"Well, yes," Maggie said.

"The last two people to live there were my cousins Ida and Imogene," Blue said. "They never said anything about a ghost. Boy, howdy, do you think it's one of them or both of them?"

"I don't know," Maggie said.

"Well, you'd know if it was Imogene, she always wore her hair in a top knot, very Kate Hepburn with the turtle-necks and the slacks," he said. "Ida was more about the flouncy dresses."

Maggie smiled. "I remember, but the presence wasn't exactly corporeal."

"Must have been Ida then, she always was the flightier of the two, having that artistic temperament and all," he said.

"I couldn't say if the presence I felt—well, more accurately, that my cat felt—was artistic or not," Maggie said.

"Wait. Hold the phone," Blue said. He held up a thin, blue-veined hand with a diamond-encrusted pinky ring. "Your cat felt a presence."

"Yes," Maggie said. She squirmed under his exasperated glare. "Marshall Dillon is very sensitive."

"How did he react?"

"He was hissing and yowling," Maggie said. "He got shut in the basement and when he came out his fur was standing on end."

"Maybe he just saw a snake or a rat," Blue said. He sounded disappointed.

"Are you telling me there are snakes and rats in the house?" Maggie asked.

Blue's eyes went wide as if he'd just remembered he was trying to sell the house to Maggie.

"No, no," he said. "I'm just speculating, you know, throwing out nonsense."

"Uh-huh," Maggie said.

"So, did you hear anything unusual?" Blue asked. "Or did you feel anything otherworldly?"

Maggie thought back to the moment she had felt a chill pass right through her. She had thought it was a draft but maybe it had been more.

"Aha!" Blue pointed at her. "You did feel something."

"A draft," Maggie said. "It was just a cold spot."

"But there weren't any doors or windows open, am I right?" Blue asked.

Maggie met his stare, and she knew he had felt the same thing she had.

"You felt it, too," she said.

"When I toured the house after it was left to me, yeah," he said. "I thought it was a draft but nothing was open."

"Is that why you never lived there?" Maggie asked.

"Nah, spirits don't bother me," he said. "Especially if it was Ida and Imogene. They loved me like a little brother, that's why they left the house to me."

"Then why not live there?"

Blue looked sly. "I'd miss all of my lady friends."

Maggie laughed. He was a charming old coot, she had to give him that.

"Do you think there is anyone else who might be haunting the house?" Maggie asked.

"The girls never mentioned it if there was," Blue said. "No, I'd say it has to be one of them. They were born in that house and died in it. It's natural they wouldn't want to leave."

"Wait, they died in it?" Maggie asked.

"Well, not 'in it,' no," he said. "Ida passed away at the county hospital after a heart attack and Imogene died a few days later of the same thing. She even had the same room, with the same time on the clock when she passed."

Maggie had heard about the sisters' demise. It had been assumed that Imogene, the caretaker of the two, had passed once Ida no longer needed her and she was free. But Maggie wondered if it was more that with Ida gone, Imogene had lost her purpose.

"I've heard that there are spirits that refuse to cross over and attach themselves to a place. Maybe Ida and Imogene were too attached to their childhood home to leave it," he said.

He sounded so matter-of-fact about it that Maggie almost started thinking it was so. She shook her head.

"Wait, I never said there was a ghost," she protested.

"Well, *you* didn't but your cat did," he argued. "Cats are especially sensitive to these things."

"Maybe it was a snake in the basement," she said.

"No, it was a ghost. It has to be," he said. "Just wait 'til I share this story with the ladies."

Maggie frowned at him. "You're just mining this for material to score with the birds."

"Now is that nice?" he asked. "Here I am, trying to help you out."

Maggie rose from her seat. "You mean you're trying to help yourself out. Listen, if you think of anything that I should know, you can always find me at my shop My Sister's Closet."

"Oh, that's yours?" he asked. "I might be in the market for a new suit."

"I have suits," Maggie said. She opened her purse and dug out a card. She handed it to him. "If you think of any family history that might be relevant, I could be persuaded to offer a discount."

"I may just take you up on that," he said. The twinkle

in his eye let Maggie know she was probably going to see Blue Dixon again and soon. "You know, you might want to talk to Ruth Crenshaw."

"The head of the historical society?"

"She knows the history of that house better than anyone."

"I hadn't thought of going over there," Maggie said. "Thanks, Mr. Dixon."

He lowered one bushy white eyebrow at her.

"I'm sorry," Maggie said with a smile. "Blue."

"That's better," he said. "Tell that fiancé of yours to stay on his toes. A fine gal like you might make a man rethink his commitment to bachelorhood."

Maggie laughed. "Now I know you're teasing me. I suspect you are perfectly content in your harem."

Blue grinned. "For now."

It suddenly became very clear to Maggie why Blue had such a horde of honeys buzzing around him.

With a wave, Maggie left him and headed into the facility. At the door, she saw two of the ladies who had been sitting with Blue eyeing her with suspicion. She flashed the diamond on her left hand just to put them at ease.

"Blue is so kind to give me and my fiancé advice on the house we're buying, isn't he?" she asked.

"Stand down, Eloise, she's not competition," the one with the pink sausage curls muttered to her companion, who had dyed her bob a severe shade of black.

"We could have taken her, Suzy," Eloise said. She gave Maggie a once-over that clearly found her wanting, and Maggie had to bite her cheek to keep from smiling.

"He is a dear man," Suzy said and she patted Maggie's arm. "You have a lovely day now."

Her polite dismissal could not have been clearer if she had held the door open and put her orthopedic shoe up against Maggie's backside.

It was a short drive from Spring Gardens to Maggie's shop. She debated stopping in at the historical society but it was time to open up and she liked to keep her hours as regular as possible.

The morning was spent haggling with Mrs. Krasinski over her Grindley china. It was a pattern discontinued in 1950. It had gold scalloped edges with purple flowers on blue vines around the edge and a burst of purple, red and blue flowers in the center. It was an eyepopper, no question.

Despite her love of all things vintage, Maggie did not love this china pattern and she seriously doubted she'd be able to sell it. Mrs. Krasinski, however, loved her wedding china and thought it was the epitome of class and good taste.

Unfortunately her son's wife had bought her own china when she got married and their two grown sons couldn't care less about china as they were just settling into married lives with young children and had no time or thought for their grandmother's precious heirlooms.

"This pattern is very exclusive," Mrs. Krasinski said as she unwrapped a salad plate from its cocoon of bubble wrap and held it out for Maggie's inspection.

The comment was unnecessary as Maggie had suffered through this discussion before. She wasn't even sure why Mrs. Krasinksi was so hot to sell the china. Her husband had left her a nice chunk of money so it wasn't as if she needed the cash. So why was she so willing to turn it over to Maggie to sell?

"Mrs. Krasinski," Maggie said. "You know my clientele is not really the china shopping sort and a full service for twelve including platters and tureens is not going to move unless I break it up."

Mrs. Krasinski gasped and put her hand over her heart as if Maggie had just blasted her with a poison dart.

"'Break it up'?"

"Not into pieces," Maggie assured her. "But into smaller lots. Instead of service for twelve, I might have better luck moving it as three sets of four."

Mrs. Krasinksi looked a little woozy. "Parcel it out? Who would get the dessert bowls? How could you divvy up the sugar bowl and creamer pitcher?"

Maggie put her hand over Mrs. Krasinksi's age-spotted one and gave it a quick, reassuring squeeze.

"Mrs. Krasinski—Eleanor—why are you trying to sell it when it is so clear that you love it?" Maggie asked.

Eleanor Krasinksi gave Maggie a wobbly smile. "I was hoping that it would prove to be of such value that my son and grandsons would reconsider and beg me not to sell it."

"So, you're hoping to incite some interest by putting fear into their hearts that they'll be losing out on a cash cow, is that it?" Maggie asked.

"Yes," Mrs. Krasinksi admitted. She gave Maggie a

sheepish look, letting her know that she knew she was being foolish. "I know it's silly, but when I picked those plates out in 1950, just before my wedding, I had a happy little daydream that one day I would be at my child's house and we would be setting the holiday dinner table with my china that I passed down."

"I don't think that's silly at all," Maggie said. "I think it's lovely."

Eleanor sighed and wrapped up her salad plate. "No, it's just an old woman's foolishness."

"Maybe," Maggie said. "But it doesn't make it any less lovely. Tell you what, how about I do some research on this pattern. Maybe we'll find out that it is exclusive, and maybe we'll have to let certain people know that their grandmother is about to sell certain pieces of their inheritance for a song."

Eleanor's eyes narrowed at Maggie. "You're sneaky."

Maggie shrugged.

"I like it," Eleanor said. "Let me know when you start the rumor so I can put my poker face on."

"Will do," Maggie said. "Oh, you'd better leave that piece with me so I can make it look authentic in case one of your grandbabies comes in here demanding to know why I'm absconding with the family china."

Eleanor looked worried and Maggie added, "I'll guard it with my life, I promise."

Eleanor carefully checked its wrapping before handing it to Maggie. "Thank you."

"No problem," Maggie said.

Eleanor Krasinski turned to leave and then she turned

back. "Oh, I nearly forgot, if you're looking for a place to pick out your china, you should go to the Lenox outlet in Dumontville. They have amazing prices, and you don't have time to dillydally. The big day is coming up, isn't it?"

Maggie felt a shiver move down her spine. "Yes, in a few weeks."

"Have you finished your registry?"

"Almost," Maggie lied. She hadn't registered for diddly-squat. "With Sam and I merging houses, there didn't seem to be a need to register for too much."

Eleanor looked appalled. "That's exactly why you *do* need to register, to start a new life together with new things so you're not just dragging the broken-down bits of your old life along with you."

Maggie frowned as she watched Eleanor leave. Broken-down bits of her old life? Is that what her miscellaneous collection of cookware and dishes represented, all that was wrong with who she had been? She had thought the years she had scraped by with her daughter, Laura, were actually some of her finest. She had learned how to make a good life for them without any of the extras.

Did she really need to throw away all of the strong and serviceable goods she had collected over the years just because she was starting a new life with Sam? Did he want her to do that? She could feel the hair on the back of her neck rising as she felt a balk coming on. This needed to be nipped in the bud and quick.

She circled the counter and put Mrs. Krasinski's plate on a shelf where it would be safe while she hatched her nefarious plan to help Eleanor out. Then she picked up the cordless phone receiver and dialed Sam's number.

"Collins," he answered.

"Do we need to register for china?" Maggie asked.

"Huh?"

"How about linens?" Maggie asked. "Do we need new sheets and towels? Whose bed are we going to use at the new house or are we going to have separate rooms?"

"No!" Sam barked.

"No, what?" Maggie asked. "No to china, linens or—"

"Separate beds," Sam interrupted. "I don't care about any of the rest of it."

"Really?"

"Really," he said. "Now explain. What's going on in that head of yours?"

"Mrs. Krasinski," Maggie said.

"Trying to unload her china again?"

"Yes, but we made progress this time," Maggie said.

"Are we getting stuck with the china?" Sam asked.

"No, but I'm going to research it and convince her grandsons that they are missing out on a veritable gold mine," she said.

"This is when I stop listening because it sounds like you are doing something illegal," he said.

"More like charitable," Maggie said. "In that I am trying to give an older lady who loves her china some peace of mind."

"That does sound like something you would do," he conceded. "So why the panic about registering?"

"Because we're getting married in a matter of weeks and I don't have a dress or a place for the reception or anything," Maggie said. "I'm a failure as a bride."

"We just bought a house," he said. "You've been busy. I bet everything falls into place now."

"I hope so," Maggie said. "I'm taking the girls over to see the house tonight. Care to meet us?"

"I can't. I'm on patrol," he said. "But while you're there, you might want to see which of our beds would fit better in the master bedroom."

His voice was low and seductive and Maggie felt her pulse kick up a notch.

"Nice to know your priorities are perfectly in order," she said.

"Natch," he agreed. "Call me later?"

"Of course," she said. "I have to tell you about my visit with Blue Dixon."

"You have been busy," he said. "Nuts, Deputy Wilson is signaling me."

"Go, you don't want Dot getting mad at you," she said.

"No, indeed, but we'll talk later," he said.

Maggie hung up, thinking Sam had sounded more like a cop than a fiancé and then realized she must be crazy in love with the man because it charmed her way more than it should have.

Chapter 5

"And this is the dining room," Maggie said as she led Ginger and Claire into the room off of the kitchen. Joanne was home with the baby and couldn't join them as she was trying to keep little Patience on a schedule.

"Oh, I like this," Ginger said. "There's plenty of room for your family and a lot of guests if you got it into your head to host a holiday dinner for your nearest and dearest."

"You don't think it's too big?" Maggie asked.

"No," Claire said. "It's perfect."

"What about the backyard?" Maggie asked. "Do you think Sam and I could keep up with that? I mean it's really big and we both work."

Ginger and Claire exchanged a look.

"All right, Maggie," Ginger said. "I've known you since

we were in kneesocks and plaid skirts and I can tell when you are waffling on a decision."

"I'm not—" Maggie protested.

"Yeah, you are," Claire said. "It's been going on since you told us about Marshall Dillon getting trapped in the basement. What we can't figure out is if you're trying to get us to talk you into loving the house or hating it. So give us a little direction here, would you?"

Maggie sighed. "I don't know."

Ginger put her arm around her friend and gave her a squeeze. "Let's approach this like we would a sale at Stegner's."

"Excellent idea," Claire said. "Let's start with the number one question: Is the price right?"

"We're getting a smoking good deal," Maggie confirmed. "It needs some work and it's been on the market for a long time."

"Will it retain its value if you decide to sell it?" Ginger asked.

"It's in the historic area of town, and if we put in the work, it could double in value," Maggie said. She felt her nerves calming a bit.

"All right, now the critical question," Claire said. "Do you need it?"

"Yes, Sam's house is a rental and my house, well, it's full of a lot of memories of a different life, you know, with Charlie and Laura. I think starting our marriage in a fresh place is wise, don't you?"

"Definitely," Claire said. "You don't want any ghosts of the past living with you and Sam."

"Funny you should mention ghosts," Maggie said. She glanced at her two friends and wondered if they were going to think she was crazy. "I think our house has one."

Ginger and Claire looked at her and then at each other. Claire laughed first and Ginger followed.

"Oh, Maggie, you are so funny," Claire said. "You almost had me going."

"Me, too," Ginger said. She waved a dismissive hand and walked back into the main living room. "Look at this place. Does it look creepy and scary to you? I mean there's not even a cobweb in sight."

"No, but—"

"And I haven't heard any strange noises like rattling chains or moaning," Claire said. "You pretty much always have to hear moaning."

"Agreed," Ginger said. "You know, it was probably just a case of buyer's panic giving you the shivers."

"You're right," Maggie said. She felt her tension ease. Thank goodness for the Good Buy Girls talking her out of her crazy spell.

"Come on, let's eat," Claire said.

They had brought a pizza and a bottle of wine with them to eat after they toured the house. Because there was no furniture, they sat on a blanket Ginger had brought in from her car and ate the pizza off paper plates and drank the wine out of paper cups picnic-style. Claire dished the pizza and Ginger poured the wine.

Maggie sat quietly, trying not to think about the cold air she felt moving in the room. *It's just a draft*, she told herself. The girls were right. The house wasn't haunted. She was just being ridiculous.

"You know what it could be," Claire said after swallowing a bite of pizza. "Wedding jitters."

"Absolutely," Ginger agreed. "You're uprooting your entire life. It is perfectly natural that you're having anxiety which has manifested itself into the idea of ghosts in your new house."

"But I'm not nervous—" Maggie began but Claire interrupted her.

"It makes perfect sense if you think about it. I mean moving and getting married are two of the three biggest life changes a person can make. Good thing you're not having a baby, too, or you'd have a trifecta of anxiety going on."

"I don't think—" Maggie began but she was interrupted by the sound of a door slamming up above.

All three of them jumped and glanced up at the ceiling.

"What was that?" Ginger hissed.

"It sounded like a door slamming," Maggie said. Her voice was faint, and she cleared her throat. "It's an old house. I suppose it could just be settling."

"Of course," Ginger said. Maggie noticed that her voice sounded a bit faint as well.

Claire forced a laugh. "Look at us. We're as jumpy as a cat in a room full of rocking chairs."

Ginger took a long sip of her wine and then laughed. "You're right. We are so lame. The boys would tease me no end if they saw me acting all scared."

Maggie glanced up at the ceiling. She couldn't shake

the feeling that this wasn't just the house settling. She didn't want to say anything that would freak the others out but she was sure she felt a presence in the house.

"You know, Sam and I never really figured out how Marshall Dillon got shut in the basement," Maggie said. "Neither one of us remembers closing the door."

"I'm sure it was just an accident," Ginger said.

Claire slowly lowered her pizza onto her plate. "Did Marshall Dillon stare past you like he could see something that wasn't there?"

"No," Maggie said.

"Did he freak out and run out of the room or try to get out of the house?" Ginger asked.

"No, he pretty much just went all big and fluffy, hissy and spitting, as he scurried past us into the room," Maggie said.

"Maybe the door was shut by a draft," Claire suggested.

"Yeah, or maybe Marcy did it, not realizing the cat was down there," Ginger said.

"Or a ghost did it," Maggie said and glanced around the room as if she was afraid of being overheard.

"Jitters, it's just wedding jitters," Claire insisted. "There is no such thing as ghosts."

Ginger nodded. "She's right. It's just your nerves. Once we get your dress and you have your cake ordered and the place for the reception nailed down, you'll feel much better."

Maggie bit a piece of pizza to keep herself from saying anything. Maybe her friends were right. Maybe she was just nervous about the wedding. The dress, if she could just nail down the dress, then she wouldn't be freaking out so much.

"You're right," she said. "I suppose I am just on anxiety overload."

"It's completely normal," Claire said.

"Absolutely, but we'll get you through it," Ginger agreed. She held up her paper cup of wine and Maggie and Claire tapped theirs against hers.

Maggie glanced around the room that would be her living room. It was a nice room. She could see herself enjoying cold winter evenings curled up on the couch reading while Sam watched his favorite sports teams and did his armchair coaching thing. The thought made her smile, and she felt herself relax.

"Okay, so what is our next move on the dress?" Ginger asked.

"I was thinking—" Maggie began but her voice trailed off as a noise from the kitchen sounded.

They all turned their heads toward the noise, which was the distinctive creak of a door opening very slowly and with great reluctance.

"House settling," Claire said. "A place this old is probably always adjusting itself."

"Right," Ginger agreed.

The lights flickered once, then twice, and the three of them looked at one another.

"Settling, my ass," Ginger said and she jumped to her feet.

A door slammed upstairs again and Claire shrieked. She and Maggie hopped to their feet as well. Claire moved to pick up the pizza box but Ginger grabbed her hand and said, "Leave it!"

A moan sounded and Maggie felt the hair on the back of her neck stand on end.

"Go! Go! Go!" she yelled. Ginger led the way with Claire behind her and Maggie following, only pausing to grab the open bottle of wine.

They ran out of the house, across the porch and down the front walk, not stopping until they were standing on the sidewalk in front of the house, huffing and puffing as they tried to catch their breath.

"Lord-a-mercy, girl." Ginger was the first to speak. "You have a ghost."

Maggie looked at her friends. They were both wide-eyed and gasping for breath. She knew she probably looked the same.

"I have to tell Sam," she said. "We can't live here. We can't live in a house with a ghost."

"What if it's a mean ghost?" Claire asked. "You could be possessed or it might make one of you kill the other."

Maggie felt all of her insides twitch in full-on panic. "Do you think it's evil? Did you get that feeling?"

Ginger put her hands on her hips while she considered. "No, I didn't get that feeling, but we were moving out of there so fast, I don't know that I would have noticed if it was a benevolent spirit or not. And really, if it is nice, why is it banging around so much?"

"And flickering off the lights is a totally passive-aggressive thing to do," Claire said.

Maggie turned to look at the house she'd been planning

to call home. The porch was wide and welcoming. She knew exactly where she wanted to put the porch swing. She'd had daydreams about her and Sam sitting on it, sharing a pitcher of lemonade on a hot summer afternoon.

The wind whipped down the street, tossing her hair about her head. A glance at the sky and the ominous clouds of an incoming storm got her feet moving toward the car.

"Come on, let's get out of here," Maggie said.

"Aren't you going to lock the door?" Claire asked her.

Maggie looked at her and then the house. "I am not going back there. You two go home. I have to talk to Sam."

Ginger nodded as if this was the most sensible thing Maggie had said all evening.

"Call us later," Claire said. "I'm going to stop by the library on my way home. I bet I can find some information on exorcisms."

Maggie gave her a faint smile. She had a feeling she was going to need something stronger than an exorcism spell. Especially when she told Sam they definitely had a ghost, and she was not moving into the house. Yeah, she was going to need a calm-the-heck-down spell.

Chapter 6

"What are you doing here?" Sam asked. He was sitting at his desk, working through a pile of paperwork, and his eyebrows shot up on his forehead when she appeared in his doorway. "And why are you carrying around an open bottle of wine?"

"To calm my nerves," Maggie said.

"What nerves?" Sam asked.

"These," Maggie said. She held out her hand so he could see her fingers trembling.

"Whoa," Sam said. He came from around his desk and held out his hand to take the bottle from her. Then he opened his arms and pulled her close.

Maggie gripped him tightly as if his warmth could chase away her fears. It almost worked.

"What happened?" Sam asked. "I thought you were meeting Ginger and Claire at the new house for a picnic?"

"We met," she said. "Then doors banged and creaked, lights flashed off then on then off then on . . ."

She paused, knowing that what she was about to say was going to sound insane. She really couldn't blame Sam if he didn't believe her. Then again, she had witnesses, so he couldn't totally dismiss what she was about to tell him.

"Then what?" he asked. He stepped back to study her face. The concern in his eyes just about undid her, but Maggie forced herself to tough it out.

"Then the ghost began moaning," she said. "Moaning as in really unhappy sounding moans as in 'get out of my house before I hurt you' moans. Sam, we can't buy that house."

He blinked at her. "Moaning?"

"Yes," she said. "Moaning as in groaning. You know, *Oooooh*, that sort of thing."

Sam propelled her toward the nearest chair. "Are you all right? Did you hit your head on anything lately? Have you eaten today? You know you go a little sideways when you haven't eaten."

"No and yes," she said. "I am not suffering from a head injury and I ate a huge lunch and was in fact just enjoying a slice of pizza when the haunting started. If you don't believe me, call Ginger and Claire, they heard it, too."

"Oh, I believe you heard something," he said. "A storm has been rolling toward us all day, bits and pieces of it have sprung up with rain and high winds right about the time you all were in the house."

"It was not wind," Maggie said. "Can wind make the lights flicker?"

"Sure, if the lines are old, and the ones to our house are," he said. "Probably, the wind is also what caused you to hear the door slam."

"Fine, but the moaning was not wind," Maggie argued.

"If it got into one of the vents or maybe a rush of air swept down the chimney, it could sound like moaning," Sam said. "Listen, we're buying a very old house. I'm sure it has tons of drafts. We're going to have to plug them all until we get the place seaworthy again."

"*Seaworthy* doesn't work for me," Maggie said. "I'm telling you that place is haunted, and it would do well to be shoved to the bottom of the ocean."

Sam gave her a small smile. "It's not haunted. You're just having a new homeowner freak-out and you're transferring your anxiety to the house."

"No, I'm not," Maggie said. "There is clearly a presence there. Even Marshall Dillon felt it."

"Marshall Dillon got locked in the basement," Sam said. "You know he hates to feel left out. I'm sure that's why he was strange the day we toured the house."

"Let's bring him back there and see," Maggie said.

"Will that make you feel better?" Sam asked.

"Only if he's calmer this time," she said. "If he freaks out, I am telling you the deal is off."

"You do realize Marcy will have a nervous breakdown if we back out of the sale now."

"I'd rather deal with Marcy's meltdown than live with a ghost freaking me out every day," she said. "This is probably why she hasn't been able to sell it: because people can sense these things."

"Maggie, let me ask you this, do you like the house?" Sam asked. He leaned against his desk and looked at her with what Maggie considered his cop face. He was looking for the truth, and she was fine with giving it to him.

"I love the house," she said. Truth. "I love the idea of the two of us spending our lives together in that beautiful old place, but I do not want to share it with anyone else, most especially anyone that we haven't invited who might, you know, be dead."

"Darling, there's no such thing as ghosts," he said.

"I know what I heard," Maggie said. "It was not the wind."

"Fine," he said. "I'll prove it to you."

"Great," she said. "How?"

"Tonight you and I are going to have a sleepover," he said. "In the new house."

Maggie gasped but Sam held up his hand, halting her protests.

"It's the only way," he said. "Go home and pack. Marshall Dillon and I will pick you up as soon as I'm done here."

Maggie thought maybe she shouldn't have been so hasty to dismiss Claire's idea of researching an exorcism. A whole night in the house? Yikes! Then she glanced at Sam and saw the challenge in his eyes. Maggie was never one to back down from a dare.

"All right, you're on, but if you can't find a rational explanation for every single noise, we call off buying the house," she said. She held out her hand. "Deal?"

"Deal," Sam said. Instead of shaking her hand, he grabbed it and used it to pull her close. "This is how you seal a bargain with your future husband."

He kissed her with a longing that made her brain turn to goo. Maggie realized she could become a betting sort of woman if this was how a wager was placed.

Marshall Dillon looked about as thrilled as Maggie to be back in the house. She stood in the living room holding him while Sam arranged their sleeping bags in front of the fire. Maggie was pleased to see that he had brought thick foam mattresses to go under the sleeping bags. She wasn't a huge fan of the whole hard-floor-as-her-pillow thing.

"Marshall Dillon does not seem happy," she said.

"He'll be fine. Go ahead and put him down," Sam said.

Maggie gently lowered the cat to the floor. She could have sworn the M on his forehead lowered in alarm but she couldn't be sure since he bolted for Sam's sleeping bag and climbed right inside of it. He peered out from under the edge, looking spooked. It was all the proof Maggie needed and she was ready to call it a night, but Sam shook his head at her and she knew he had read her mind.

"The house is not haunted," Sam said. They had put several pillar candles in the fireplace to give the room some ambiance, but the shadows the candles threw up on the walls made Maggie skittish.

"Come here," Sam said.

He held out his arm and Maggie scooted under it. He kissed her temple and together they leaned back against their pillows and stared at the candles flickering in the brick fireplace. Cuddled up like this Maggie could almost believe that the house was fine, that it had just been the wind, but then she remembered the flickering lights.

No, there was something more going on here, and Sam just needed to see it for himself.

"Let's talk about something happy," Sam said. "That'll take your mind off of your worries."

"All right," Maggie said. She settled her back against Sam's front and despite her misgivings, she felt safe and secure as if nothing could harm her while she had Sam nearby.

"Where are we going to have the wedding reception?" Sam asked.

Maggie groaned. "I thought you said we were going to talk about something happy."

"Our wedding reception isn't happy?" he asked.

"Your mother wants it in the church hall," Maggie said.

"She said that?" Sam asked.

"She sent me a text letting me know it was available," Maggie said. "At the same time my mother sent me a text recommending the gazebo in the town green."

"What if it rains?" Sam asked.

"That was your mother's point," Maggie said.

"But it might not," Sam said.

"Which was my mother's point," Maggie said.

"Maybe we could hire the two of them," Sam said.

Maggie frowned. "My mother wants our cake to be strawberries and cream while your mother is lobbying for white chocolate raspberry."

"How about we have chocolate?" Sam asked.

"Now you're talking my language," Maggie said. "But then we have to choose what goes on top of the cake."

"You mean other than frosting?" Sam asked. He sounded confused, and it made Maggie smile.

"Yes, we have to decide if we're going to have the little bride and groom statue or just flowers or live doves or whatever," Maggie said.

"Live doves might poop on the cake," Sam said. "I vote for flowers."

"What kind?"

"I hear calla lilies are pretty," he said.

"You almost brought me a bouquet of those once," Maggie said. "But they never arrived."

"No, I chickened out, because I was afraid to get my heart trampled again," he said. "Let's go with the calla lilies. I chose them that day because the florist told me they stand for rebirth."

"As in a second chance?" Maggie asked.

"I'd like to think we're making the most of our second time around," he said.

"Agreed," she said. "Calla lilies it is."

"What else do the moms have an opinion on?" he asked.

"My hair, whether I should wear it up or down," she said.

"Down," Sam said. "Next."

Maggie turned to look at him. "You're kind of being bossy. Why does my hair need to be down?"

"Because when we were in school and I sat behind you in Mr. Meehan's seventh grade biology class, I used to stare at your hair for hours," he said. "It isn't just one color, you know."

"Red isn't one color?" she asked.

"Not on you," he said. "I always thought your hair was magical because I could see blond strands, copper strands and streaks of color that defied description but were as amazing to look at as honey shot with amber."

Maggie frowned at the hair that hung over her shoulder. It was auburn, a nice plain red with some brown and blond mixed in, but mostly it was red. She couldn't help but be flattered by Sam's description, however. Given that he used to call her "Carrots" when they were kids, she certainly appreciated how much his view of her had changed.

"Well, since you feel so strongly about it, the hair is down," she said.

"See how much we're getting done with the wedding?" he asked. "What else?"

"My dress," Maggie said. "I don't have a dress."

"You'll find one," Sam said.

"I don't want to wear white," Maggie said. "It seems silly since I have a grown daughter and all."

"Darling, you could show up in a plastic garbage sack and still be the most beautiful woman in the room," he said. "It's your day, wear whatever you want."

"Careful, I may just take you up on that," she said. "What about you? Suit or tux?"

"My mother has been lobbying for a tux," he said. "My brothers have been pushing for Hawaiian shirts and a backyard barbeque."

"I like the way they think," Maggie said. "But I'm glad to see you're getting squeezed by your loved ones as well."

"It does seem like everyone has an opinion about our wedding. Except for the bride that is," he said. He shifted Maggie so that he could see her face. His gaze was scrutinizing—his detective's expression—when he looked at her. "Is there something you want to talk about?"

"What do you mean?" she asked.

"Are you having second thoughts?" he asked.

"What? No!" she insisted. "What makes you think that?"

"Let's see, we're a few weeks from our wedding and you seem undecided about everything and we've just bought a house that you are certain is haunted. It all makes me think maybe you're just not ready for marriage and a house, or more accurately, a life together."

His face was calm. There was no accusation or hurt showing on his handsome features, but Maggie knew Sam Collins and she knew his tough guy exterior would never let him show it if he was feeling hurt by her waffling.

"Oh, Sam," she said. She placed her hand on the side of his face and stared into his eyes so he would know the truth of her words. "I am absolutely positive that I want to spend the rest of my life with you."

"But," he prodded.

"But there are just so many decisions to be made," she said. "I'm not a big fan of change. I mean leaving Doc Franklin's to open my shop was the biggest change I'd made in forever and I sort of thought it would be the last. Then you came along . . ."

"And blew that all to heck," he said with a grin.

"In the best possible way, yes," she agreed. "I will find the right dress and I will nail down the details, I promise."

"I can help," he said. "Anything you need, even if it's taking on the moms, I can make it work. You know the only thing that matters is that we're making a lifetime commitment to each other. The rest is just details."

Maggie smiled as she relaxed against him. Sam was right. What mattered most was right here in this room.

"Feel better?" he asked.

"I do," she said. Then she laughed. "See? *I do* flies right out of my mouth when I'm with you."

Sam gave her a solid squeeze. "Good. Now, about the house, nothing strange has happened and we've been here for two hours. Even Marshall Dillon has calmed down. How are you feeling about this place?"

Maggie glanced around the room. It felt cozy instead of creepy, and at that moment, she had a hard time believing that there could be a presence haunting them.

Maybe Ginger and Claire had been right from the very beginning, maybe she was just having wedding jitters. Now that she and Sam had ironed out some of the wedding wrinkles, she was feeling very peaceful about the whole matrimony thing and that included the house as well. She and Sam could have a very happy life here together. She was sure of it.

"You're right," she said. "Nothing weird has happened. It must have been my imagina—"

The sound of floorboards creaking overhead as if someone were running down the hallway interrupted what Maggie had been about to say.

She glanced at Sam, who was frowning.

"Wind?" Maggie asked. Her voice was just above a whisper.

"Maybe," Sam said. His voice sounded grim.

A door slammed. The creaking floorboards sounded again. A soft moan broke through the quiet, making Maggie's skin prickle. The lights went out.

"Or maybe not," Sam said.

Chapter 7

Maggie shivered. The only light in the room came from the candles they had lit in the fireplace. As if sensing her upset, Marshall Dillon left his cocoon in the sleeping bag and jumped into her lap.

Sam went over to the light switch on the wall. He flicked the switch. Nothing happened.

He crossed over to his bag on the floor and rifled through it until he pulled out a flashlight. He switched it on and the beam illuminated the dark corner of the room.

"Stay here," he said.

"Do you even know me?" she asked.

In the candlelight, she saw him grin.

"Yeah, what was I thinking?" he asked. "Come on."

Maggie tucked Marshall Dillon under the crook of

her arm and followed Sam. Instead of going upstairs, however, he headed for the door that led to the basement.

"Whoa, whoa, whoa." She balked. "The noise came from upstairs."

"Yes, but the fuse box, where we control the electricity, is downstairs," he said. "I'm sure the wind just tripped a circuit breaker or maybe we blew a fuse. Either way, wouldn't you rather investigate upstairs with the lights on?"

"Good point," she said. "Lead the way."

The basement was unfinished. They had toured it in daylight, and Maggie remembered the dank smell and rough floor. It had been empty except for the oil furnace, a shelf of old empty canning jars and a collection of rusty tools that were now relics more than anything else.

Sam led the way. The wooden steps groaned beneath his feet and it made Maggie wonder how a ghost, who would conceivably weigh nothing, could make a floor creak. Did that mean there was a person in the house with them? Maybe someone didn't want them to buy the house and was trying to spook them out. This didn't make her feel much better than the idea of a ghost being in the house, but at least if it was a person, Sam could arrest them.

The thought of someone terrorizing them made Maggie mad. If someone else wanted the house, they should have bought it and not tried to scare the snot out of people, namely her.

Marshall Dillon wriggled in her arms as she followed Sam down the steps. With a yowl, he sprang from her grasp and bolted back up the steps into the house.

"Marshall Dillon!" she cried.

Sam turned on the steps and shone the flashlight after the cat.

"Everything okay?" he asked.

"Marshall refused to go into the basement," Maggie said. "I think he's headed back to his sleeping bag."

"He'll be all right," Sam said.

"Do you think he senses a presence?" Maggie asked.

"No," Sam said. His tone was dry. "I'm betting he sensed a draft and decided his sleeping bag was much more comfortable."

As if to emphasize Sam's words, a chill wind blew through the basement and Maggie shivered.

"Come on, I'll need you to hold the flashlight for me." Sam put his arm around her shoulders and led her to the far end of the basement.

He handed the flashlight to Maggie and she shined the beam at the rectangular gray metal box. Sam flipped it open and began to study the switches. Maggie had been on her own long enough to know what all the black levers meant. Still, she preferred to call an electrician when she had issues since she had a healthy fear of electrocuting herself.

"Huh," Sam muttered as he examined the box.

Maggie shifted from foot to foot. She glanced over her shoulder. Was something moving in the shadows? She snapped the flashlight in that direction. It was empty.

"Darling, I can't see much without light."

"Did you see that?" Maggie said. "I swear I saw something moving in the shadows."

Sam stepped beside her and stared at the place where she pointed the flashlight. "Nope."

"There was something there," she said. She knew she sounded defensive but she couldn't help it. She could feel the hair on the back of her neck prickling and she couldn't shake the feeling that someone was watching them.

"You do realize this is a perfect backdrop for a horror movie, don't you?" she asked.

She didn't resist when he pulled the flashlight out of her hands.

"Stay close," he said. "I promise I won't let any masked slasher leap out of the shadows and shank us."

"Not helping," she said.

"Sorry."

Given that Sam's attention was completely on the fuse box, Maggie felt that his apology was a half effort at best. She pressed closer to him, trying to absorb some of his warmth. Despite the fact that it was June in Virginia, the basement was cold.

"Well, that's weird," Sam said.

"What? Did you see something?" Maggie asked.

"Yeah, someone switched off the electricity to the living room," he said. He flipped a switch and looked at Maggie. "That should do it."

"Wait, hold up," Maggie said. "What do you mean someone switched it off?"

Sam began to walk toward the cellar storm doors. "Do you remember if these doors had a lock?"

"No," Maggie said. "I don't think I spent much time

thinking about the basement. Why? What do you think happened?"

Sam moved back by the stairs where the lone light in the basement was located. He pulled the string and the environmentally friendly lightbulb shone brightly in the darkness. He switched off the flashlight.

"It could be we had a squatter using the basement," Sam said. He crossed back over to the storm doors and examined them and the steps leading up and out of the basement into the side yard.

"A squatter?" Maggie asked.

"Could be. If these doors were kept unlocked, it would give a vagrant access to the house," Sam said.

He pushed one of the doors open and popped his head outside. Then he reappeared, letting the door bang shut behind him.

"The place has been empty for five years. It could be that someone or maybe a couple of someones have been staying in the house while it was vacant."

"Do you think they're the ones who switched off the lights to the living room?"

"Could be," he said. "If there is more than one of them, one could have been downstairs tampering with the lights while the other one made the noise upstairs that scared you and the girls earlier."

"Well, that's just mean," Maggie said. She was feeling more irritated by the minute.

Sam shrugged. "They haven't done any damage and this place has given them shelter. It's hard to blame them for not wanting to give up their home."

"Okay, I'll give you that. But we're going to lock the storm doors, right?"

"Yes," Sam said. "I don't want you getting scared again. Here. Let's see if we can find a board or something to put through the handles to keep the doors shut."

Maggie went one way and Sam the other. With the light on, the basement was still dank and musty but no longer scary. Sam found a rake handle but it was too long to fit. Maggie found some rope but it was too rotten to use.

While Sam dug through the rusty pile of tools, Maggie looked at the boards holding up the canning jars. Surely one of those would fit. She took the jars off the top shelf and put them along the wall to the side of the makeshift shelving unit. She tried to lift off the top board but it had been nailed to the two side boards. The only way to take it apart was to pull down all of the canning jars.

"Any luck?" she asked Sam.

"Not yet," he answered.

Maggie turned back to the jars covered in dirt and grime. With a sigh, she continued moving them. At last the stubby shelf was free and she pulled it clear of the wall.

"If we can break this apart," she called to Sam, "it might work."

He had the head of an axe in his hand and he grinned. "I think I found just the tool for that. Stand clear."

Maggie moved back to the wall while Sam banged at the shelves with the axe head. She had thought the canning jars were up against the wall but as she looked more closely she realized that they had been propped up in front of a small wooden door.

The handle on the door was old and rusty. Maggie pushed the thumb lever down and put some pressure on the door. To her surprise it moved. She shoved it wide and jumped back just in case any nasties such as snakes, rats, bats or spiders had made their home in the tiny root cellar and were unhappy at being disturbed.

Nothing leapt out of the dark hole but she wasn't about to go in without light. She hurried across the cellar and grabbed the flashlight Sam had left by the circuit breaker box. She switched it on and shined the beam into the root cellar. It looked empty, which she supposed was a blessing given that she didn't want to be the proud owner of a bunch of old jars full of botulism.

She pointed the beam down to the floor and swept it across the small space. The light winked off of something shiny and she paused. She moved the beam over the floor again and gasped.

"Sam!" she cried. He was still banging on the wooden shelves and she was forced to shout. "Sam!"

He paused. Something in her tone must have alerted him to her upset.

"What is it, darling?"

"I think I found our ghost," she said.

Chapter 8

"What?" Sam raced to her side. He glanced at where she pointed the beam of light. "Is that a—"

"Skeleton?" Maggie asked. "Yes, I'm pretty sure it is."

"Stay here," Sam said. He took the flashlight and climbed into the small root cellar. Maggie followed. He gave her a quick glance and she shrugged.

"I found it," she said.

"Fine, but don't touch anything," he said.

The tiny root cellar was too small for them to stand in so they crouched low. Sam ran the beam of light over the body and Maggie saw that what had glinted in the light before was a medal. It was pinned to the olive drab jacket that the skeleton was still wearing. So, he had been a soldier.

Maggie leaned over the body, trying to see where there might be a name stitched onto the uniform. The material was rotten and full of holes; the only thing holding it together was the medal pinned to the remnants of the fabric.

The white gleam of the skeleton's bones shone through the ratty fabric of the old uniform. Maggie forced herself to look at the head. The skull with its vacant eye sockets and leering grin made her shiver.

"You okay?" Sam asked.

"Yeah, sure," Maggie lied. She didn't want to be wimpy but her imagination was running overtime. "Do you think he was murdered?"

Sam glanced around the room and then at Maggie. "Well, I don't imagine he chose to die in here."

"No, I suppose not," she said. She had been hoping he'd have an alternate idea but there really was no arguing with the fact that the soldier was in a root cellar and had been for a mighty long time.

"Come on," Sam said. "I think this is going to take a special skill set and I know just the person to call."

"Who?" Maggie asked as she took Sam's hand and let him lead her out of the tiny space.

"A colleague of mine: Andy Lowenstein, a forensic pathologist I worked with in Richmond."

"Excellent. So, do you think we found our ghost?" Maggie asked.

"We don't have a ghost," Sam said. He looked grumpy.

As they approached the stairs, Maggie heard the

sound of creaking floorboards above and she turned to look at Sam as if this proved her case.

"You sure about that?" she asked.

Sam pushed around her and took the stairs at a run.

"If there is someone up there, this time I'm going to catch them."

He took the stairs two at a time. Maggie scurried up behind him, having no desire to stay downstairs in the cellar with the skeleton.

Sam was jogging through the house and Maggie was hot on his heels. A door slammed upstairs and Sam flicked on the lights, which worked, and ran up the staircase.

Again, Maggie had no desire to be left behind so she followed him up to the second floor. The only door that was shut was the one to the master bedroom. Sam pushed it open and snapped on the overhead light. The room was empty.

A stiff breeze blew in through an open window. Sam crossed the room and peered out through the old casement to the ground below.

Maggie squeezed in beside him to look outside. There was nothing but a bare expanse of lawn. The large mulberry tree was set far enough away from the house that no one except Spiderman could have jumped for it and made it.

"Ghost," she said to Sam. "It has to be."

"There are no such things as ghosts," he argued. "I know the idea is fun and spooky but there has never been any evidence to indicate that ghosts are real."

"Really?" Maggie asked. "Then how do you explain all of this?"

"The wind, a vagrant, a large stray cat or maybe our cat," Sam said. He closed the window and latched it. He turned to look at her when he was finished. "It was not a ghost."

"But we have a skeleton," Maggie protested. "Surely, if we have a skeleton, we could have a ghost."

"Is this opinion based on scientific evidence?" Sam asked. He crossed the room, scanning it as he went. "'Cause I'm pretty sure Doc Franklin would agree with me and say there is no such thing as ghosts."

"You'd be surprised," Maggie said. "That man has sat at the bedside of a lot of patients who have crossed over and he has a pretty unique perspective on death."

"Does he now?" Sam said. "Well, I hate to break it to him and you, but ghosts don't exist. Period."

The thundering sound of footsteps running on hardwood sounded below and Maggie jumped. Sam frowned.

"That'll be Marshall Dillon chasing a mouse," Sam said.

"Mouse?" Maggie cried. "I'd rather have a ghost."

Sam grinned and wrapped his arm around her shoulders.

"Come on, ghost hunter, I have some calls to make," he said.

When they entered the living room, sure enough, Marshall Dillon was scampering around the room, looking as if he was having the time of his life. There was no hair up on his back and he wasn't hissing or spitting. Instead he was chasing a string from one of the sleeping bags across the floor.

"See?" Sam asked. "No ghost."

"Maybe," Maggie said. "Or maybe Marshall just made friends with it. I mean it must be lonely, haunting an abandoned house for the past five years with no one to keep it company."

Sam made a face palm and Maggie hid her smile. Why did she enjoy needling him so much? Oh yeah, 'cause she loved him.

Sam peeked at her between his fingers. "You're enjoying this, aren't you?"

"It's keeping me calm as opposed to freaking out because the house we just bought, that we are planning to spend the rest of our lives in, has a dead body in the basement," she said.

"It's a skeleton," he corrected. "The body is long gone."

"And that makes it better how?" she asked.

"Rotting flesh versus bleached bones," Sam said. "Bones win every time, mostly because of the lack of an odor."

"Okay, okay, I'm sorry I asked," she said. "What do we do now?"

"I'm going to stay with Bones," he said. "And you're going to go home and get some rest."

"Bones? Really?" she asked.

"He needs a name," he said. "John Doe seems unimaginative given the situation."

"How about Captain Bones, since he was clearly a military pilot," Maggie said. "As he had the appropriate wings on the front of his jacket. Well, what was left of it."

"You noticed?" Sam asked in approval. "Good eye. Captain Bones it is. I'm going to call the county medical examiner in the morning and have him meet me here. There's not much point in rousing him tonight, but I'll stay and keep an eye on things."

"You're going to stay here all alone?" Maggie asked.

"Captain Bones will keep me company," he said.

"But it's so creepy," Maggie protested. "I don't like the idea of you here alone at night. I'll stay and we can take turns keeping watch."

"What if you see the ghost?" Sam asked. His tone was teasing but Maggie pretended it wasn't.

"I will scream my fool head off," she said. "But since you're so sure there's no such thing as ghosts, I should be just fine and not ruin your sleep."

"Why do I get the feeling you're mocking me?" he asked.

Maggie gave him her most innocent look. He frowned. Clearly he was not buying what she was selling.

"Come on, it'll be fun," she said. "Like camping out in a graveyard."

"I thought you were afraid," he said.

"That's before I knew what we were dealing with," Maggie said. "Obviously, our ghost is the soldier in the basement and I think if we identify him and give him a proper send-off, he will abandon the premises and our house will be all clear of spectral phenomena."

Sam looked at her. "You know you sound nuts, right?"

"Listen," Maggie said. Sam looked at her, and she shook her head. "No, not to me, listen to the house." They both did. There was nothing but silence. "See? Since we found the body and have decided to figure out who he is, there's been no creaking, moaning or door slamming."

"So, you still want to live here?" Sam asked.

"Now more than ever," Maggie said. "It'll be like doing a good deed before we move in. Excellent karma."

"And if it was the wind?" Sam asked.

"We'll fix the drafts," she said.

Sam pulled her close, gave her a solid squeeze and kissed the top of her head.

"All right," he said. "You want first watch?"

Maggie glanced around the room to where Marshall Dillon lay curled up in her sleeping bag.

"Yeah, that sounds good," she said.

Sam climbed into his sleeping bag, and the cat—the traitor—got up, stretched and climbed in with him. Maggie positioned herself so she could see the cellar door. She wasn't sure why, since Sam had blocked off the storm doors in the basement so no one could get in, and it wasn't likely that Captain Bones was going to jog up the stairs to join them. Still, she felt better with her eyes on that door just in case.

The mere thought of the skeleton coming upstairs made her shiver.

"You all right?" Sam asked.

"Just fine," Maggie lied. "Go to sleep."

"Come here," he said. He lifted his arm and pulled Maggie close. "We can do the first watch together."

Maggie didn't want to admit how much better this made her feel, but it did. She wasn't ready to face the ghost that inhabited their house by herself. And yes, even though she had told Sam she thought it was at peace now that they'd found its skeleton, she wasn't 100% sure it wouldn't rouse itself to scare them again. From what she'd heard and read ghosts were mercurial beings—or nonbeings as it were.

She nestled close to Sam and listened to his heartbeat. It was slow and steady without a hint of anxiety. Before Maggie knew it, she was lulled to sleep like a puppy cozied up to the ticktock of a clock.

Morning brought the arrival of the county medical examiner along with Deputy Dot Wilson, who was Sam's favorite St. Stanley police department employee, although he never admitted it.

Maggie and Marshall Dillon were sitting on the back porch of the house, trying to stay out of the way, when Dot poked her head out the back door.

"Morning, Maggie," Dot greeted her.

A short, well-endowed black woman with a badge, Dot walked into every room like she owned it. Probably it was the shoes. She had a thing for shoes and had a standing order with Maggie that anything Maggie got in the shop that was Italian in a size seven was to be put aside for her. Maggie noted that Sam had never called Dot on her non-regulation footwear, which sort of proved the whole favoritism thing.

"Morning, Dot," Maggie said. She waved toward the kitchen. "There's coffee on if you want."

"Thanks but I had the night shift," Dot said. "I'm actually on my way home to sleep."

"Oh, that sounds good," Maggie said.

She had conked out early during the first watch but had woken up in the middle of the night and pulled a shift all by herself. Of course, *she* had been on the alert for ghosts, while Sam had been looking for squatters. Either way, neither of them had gotten much shut-eye given the discomfort of the hard floor coupled with the anxiety of finding a skeleton in their basement.

Maggie couldn't help but wonder how the poor soldier had gotten down there. Could it have had something to do with his military career? Maybe he had gone AWOL and gotten trapped in the root cellar and died. Or maybe it had been an accident? Maybe he got drunk and crawled in there to sleep it off but then a poisonous snake bit him and he died.

Or maybe it had been murder. But who would kill a soldier—a captain, no less—and hide his body in a root cellar? The questions had spun around in Maggie's head all night long and she knew Sam had suffered the same.

Dot sat down on the top step beside Maggie. With her uniform, she was wearing a pair of dark gray Donald J Pliner booties that had chunky heels and Maggie was quite certain had not come from her shop.

"Tell me you did not pay retail for those," Maggie said.

"No, they were on sale," Dot said. "Now about—"

"Oh no you don't," Maggie said. "Where were they on sale?"

"Aw, what?" Dot asked. "You're quizzing me about shoes now?"

"Where'd you get them, Dot?"

"SecondTimeAround," Dot mumbled the words together as if Maggie couldn't decipher her rival's shop name.

"You bought them from Summer?" Maggie cried. "Ah, the betrayal!"

"She gave me 70% off," Dot said. "You cannot hold that against me."

"Ugh, I guess not," Maggie said, but it was grudging.

"Long night, huh?" Dot asked.

"Yeah, I'm sorry I'm being cranky. Nice score on the boots," Maggie said. Dot nodded in acknowledgment. "Has the medical examiner said anything?"

"No, they're down in the basement, taking pictures and trying to find evidence," Dot said. "The first thing they'll have to do is get an ID on the vic."

"Vic?" Maggie asked. "So they think it was a murder?"

"Seems so, I mean the guy is in a root cellar," Dot said. "No one winds up a skeleton in a root cellar by choice."

Chapter 9

"Agreed," Maggie said. "I was thinking I'd pop in over at the historical society and see what information they have about the house. Blue Dixon said I should talk to Ruth Crenshaw about, well, if there could be a ghost here."

"Ruth would know," Dot agreed. "And there's definitely a ghost here."

"Deputy Wilson, do not go putting ideas into my fiancée's head," Sam said as he joined them on the porch.

"The idea was already there as well you know," Maggie said. "Dot just confirmed it."

"He doesn't believe?" Dot asked Maggie. Maggie shook her head. Dot waved her hand dismissively. "It's on account of he's a man and they don't have a woman's intuition."

"See?" Maggie said. "Dot feels it, too."

Sam rolled his eyes.

"There is nothing to feel in this house except a draft," he said.

Dot rose to her feet, clucked her tongue and shook her head at Sam. Then she turned to Maggie and said, "You'd better keep a close eye on him so he doesn't piss off our visitor from the other realm. You don't want a mad ghost on your hands. My cousin had a ghost and her husband didn't believe it and he disrespected the spirit and, oh, did he pay."

Maggie knew better than to ask and yet the words were out of her mouth before she could stop herself. "What happened?"

"My cousin says she's not sure because she was upstairs sleeping, but when she got up she found her husband, who was known for mocking their specter, face down in his Corn Flakes. He died of a heart attack right in his break-fast cereal."

"How can you blame a ghost for a man's heart attack?" Sam asked. "Heart disease is the reason most people die. One has nothing to do with the other."

"Sure it does," Dot protested. "My cousin swears that the ghost must have manifested in front of her husband and scared him to death, because he'd just had a physical and he was perfectly fine."

"Doctors miss things," Sam said. But he sounded as if he knew he'd lost the argument, or at least any hope for swaying Dot and Maggie to his side.

"Forty-three years old and in the prime of his life," Dot said. "They didn't miss anything. There were all sorts of blood tests and stress tests, the whole shebang. Say, aren't you forty-three?"

"Don't you have some place to be?" Sam asked. "Like helping the ME down in the basement?"

"No need to get testy," Dot said. "Just be nice to your ghost and you won't have to worry about keeling over into your Wheaties."

"I don't eat cereal," Sam said. "I'm a donut man."

"When you're taking a permanent nap on the jellies, don't say I didn't warn you," Dot said. She wagged her finger at Sam for good measure and Maggie could tell he was hanging onto his temper by a hair.

Dot gave him a look and left to go back into the house. Sam heaved a sigh, took the seat beside Maggie and put his arm around her and pulled her close.

"What's your plan for today?" he asked.

"Mom and Sissy are arriving," she said. She glanced at her watch. "In fact, they're probably arriving right now."

"Shouldn't you go and meet them?" Sam asked.

"Nah, they'll go straight to Sandy's house to see Josh," Maggie said. Then she grinned. "Even as a bride I can't hold a candle to that boy."

"He is pretty spectacular," Sam said.

"And he's the only great-grandchild so my mother is completely besotted with him," Maggie said.

"Do me a favor?" Sam asked.

"Sure," Maggie said.

"Don't tell your mother about your ghost theory, because then she'll call my mother," he said. "And my mother is very superstitious, and I do mean *very*."

"Will she think we should unload the house?" Maggie asked.

"More like we should burn it to the ground," he said.

"Oh," she said. "That's harsh."

"Yeah, she's a teensy bit freaked out by the idea of the supernatural," he said.

"See? This is why we need to emancipate our ghost by solving its murder," Maggie said. "I'm going to go to the historical society and see Ruth Crenshaw. I'll bet she knows who our soldier might be."

Sam nodded. "Good idea. You might want to give her a heads-up that I'll be over later to talk to her. We can compare notes. Hey, maybe she'll help us wrap up this case in no time."

"That would be very considerate of her," Maggie said. "We do have a wedding to plan after all."

"Oh no," Sam said with a shake of his head. "The wedding comes before figuring out the ghost thing."

"But how can we live here with a ghost?" Maggie asked. "We have to solve the ghost issue before we move in."

"Darling, you need to seriously rethink your priorities," Sam said. Then he kissed her. It was not the chaste peck of a man on duty, either.

When he pulled away, Maggie's ears were ringing and she was pretty sure she'd gone cross-eyed.

"You're right." She cleared her throat. "Wedding first."

"That's my girl." Sam grinned. "Come on, I'll walk you out. Be sure to give your mother my best. Is she warming up to me at all?"

"No," Maggie said. "She's still worried that you'll break my heart again."

"Seems as though she should be worried about me," Sam said.

"How do you figure?"

"We both know you're the flight risk in this relationship," he said.

"No, we don't," Maggie argued. "I completely disagree. If either of us is apt to walk, it's you."

"Me?" Sam asked. "I'm as faithful as a dog."

Maggie frowned at him. "Maybe not the best example with all of the butt sniffing they do."

"Point taken," Sam said with a laugh.

Maggie led the way back into the house. Marshall Dillon was curled up on Sam's sleeping bag, and she scooped him and held him close.

"Call me if you find out anything about Captain Bones," she said.

"Likewise," Sam said.

Maggie climbed into her Volvo station wagon, putting Marshall Dillon in his carrier in the back seat. She backed out of the driveway, pausing at the end to look up at her new home. What would they do if identifying the skeleton and figuring out how he died didn't take care of their ghost problem?

She shook her head. One problem at a time, and right now it was her mother.

* * *

"You really need to talk to Shelby at the VFW if you want to rent their hall for the reception," Maggie's mother said. "It's probably already booked but you might get lucky."

"Hello to you, too," Maggie said as she hugged her mother close.

"The entire drive up from Florida she talked about your wedding," Sissy said in her ear as she hugged Maggie next. "You owe me, Magpie."

"Fifty percent off any one buying spree at the shop," she said.

"Make it seventy-five and all is forgiven," Sissy haggled. They were not sisters for nothing.

"Sixty-five," Maggie countered.

"Seventy," Sissy said. She stepped out of the hug and turned to their mother and said, "Maggie is eloping to Vegas."

"No! What? When did you decide this?" Mrs. O'Brien put her hand over her heart as if she couldn't bear the news.

"Fine, 70%," Maggie said to her sister. "Mom, relax. Sissy is kidding. We're not eloping."

"Oh, thank goodness," her mother sighed. Then she frowned at Sissy. "That was not nice."

Sissy winked at Maggie, and Maggie couldn't help but smile. Sissy was always the prankster. It was good to have her here for the wedding.

"When is Laura arriving?" Maggie's mother asked.

"A few days before the wedding," Maggie said.

"Does she have her maid of honor dress?"

"I think so," Maggie said. "She was deciding between two different ones."

"What did they look like? What colors are they?" Mrs. O'Brien asked.

"Uh." Maggie turned to Sissy for help but Sissy held up her hands.

"Don't look at me," she said. "I was your maid of honor last time. Since you're just having Laura, I am out of the informational loop."

"I think one was green and one was blue," Maggie said.

"Well, that narrows it," Mrs. O'Brien said. "I'm going to call Laura and get more specifics. Gracious, it's a good thing we got here a few weeks early. Clearly, you need all the help you can get."

She left the room, waving her hands in the air like she was about to call in a fire.

"Oh my god," Maggie said.

"Did I mention your wedding was all she talked about for the whole ride?" Sissy asked. "You'd think it was your first wedding."

"I'm sorry," Maggie said and bit her lip.

"Forget about it," Sissy said.

"Where are the kids?" Maggie asked.

"Josh and Sandy went for a walk to the park," Sissy said. "And Jake is at work."

"Oh," Maggie said.

Sissy grinned. "You're sorry you missed seeing the boy."

"Yeah," Maggie said. "My house is so quiet since they bought this place."

Maggie glanced around the modest home that was so like her own. Her niece Sandy had done an amazing job of decorating it. She and Jake had waited a long time to be able to have a home of their own, since he had been away on a tour of duty in Afghanistan. Maggie was happy for them even though she missed the commotion of having Josh and Sandy living with her.

"I'm just glad Sandy had you while she finished nursing school and waited for Jake to come home," Sissy said. "I owe you for that."

"Nah, that's what family is for," Maggie said. "Besides you took Mom to live with you in Florida. I'd say I got the better end of the bargain."

Sissy nodded. "There are days. Want some lemonade? I want to hear more about this house you and Sam have bought."

"Oh, I wish I could, but I have to go and open up the shop," Maggie said as she backed to the door. "And I have some errands to run. I will tell you about the house later, though, I promise."

"You do not fool me one little bit, Magpie," Sissy chided her. "You're avoiding Mom and her wedding talk."

"Me?" Maggie asked as she slipped through the screen door. "I can't imagine what you mean."

She heard Sissy laugh as the door swung shut behind her. With a wave, she climbed into her car and headed into town. She had dropped off Marshall Dillon at Sam's house before she'd headed home to shower and change. The quick pop in at Sandy's to see her mother had gone more smoothly than she'd anticipated, mostly because she had thrown her daughter's dress dilemma at her like a bone to a dog. But she could live with that.

She glanced at the clock on her dashboard: She had just enough time to stop by the historical society before opening her shop for the day. She wasn't really sure of what she was looking for but anything about the Dixons or the house seemed like a good place to start.

The St. Stanley Historical Society was housed in an old wooden building in the center of town. The small structure had once been a telegraph office but had been abandoned and stayed empty for a decade before someone on the ladies' auxiliary got the bright idea to turn it into the town's historical society. It sat on the corner of the town green tucked behind the new addition to the library.

The historical society kept bankers' hours, open from nine to five during the week and nine to noon on Saturdays. Maggie generally opened her store at ten, so she had just enough time to pop in and get some books about the Dixon house and any other information she could find before she had to hustle over to her store.

Maggie pulled open the green door with the large glass pane in its center. The smell of aged paper and peaches scented the air with a pleasant bouquet that reminded her of summer afternoons spent in her grandmother's attic with Sissy, playing dress up in their grandmother's old clothes. It was one of those happy memories that filled her up on the inside and made her smile.

She glanced at the desk in the center of the room. It was vacant. The building consisted of two small rooms on the first floor and an upstairs office. The wooden floorboards creaked when she stepped across them and Maggie thought someone must have heard her come in. No one came out front, however.

She cleared her throat and called, "Hello! Is anyone here?"

She waited a moment and then heard the sound of footsteps lightly moving across the floor above. Maggie glanced up, wondering if whoever was up there had heard her.

A tiny woman with the fragile build of a sparrow peeked around the doorframe at the top of the stairs. Seeing Maggie, her eyes went wide behind her large-framed glasses and she hurried down the steps.

"I wondered when you'd stop by," Ruth Crenshaw said.

Ruth Crenshaw, self-appointed town historian, was an original. She wore her long gray hair in a braid that hung halfway down her back. Her fashion sense was sensible brown shoes, thick stockings, flouncy skirts with big, bold flowers on them and puffy-sleeved blouses that she wore buttoned up to her throat. Her makeup consisted of two dots of blush on her gaunt cheeks and a brightly painted mouth. Occasionally she busted out the blue eye shadow but that was mostly for special occasions.

"Hi, Ruth," Maggie said. "What made you think I would be stopping in?"

Maggie wondered if Sam had already spoken to Ruth and, if so, how much he had told her.

"Well, you bought the Dixon house, so I knew it was just a matter of time."

"'Matter of time'?" Maggie repeated her, feeling as if she had walked into the middle of the conversation.

"Yes," Ruth said. She sucked on her teeth and studied Maggie from behind the big lenses of her glasses. "You know, until you learned the house's secret."

Chapter 10

Maggie felt her eyebrows shoot up. Did Ruth know about the skeleton? Or did she know about the ghost and, if so, how?

"Don't look so surprised," Ruth chided her. "All houses have secrets."

"I suppose," Maggie said. "Mostly, I was just looking for any history about the residents of the house. You know, the Dixon family."

"Why?" Ruth asked. She stared at Maggie with the unnerving unblinking stare of an owl watching a fat rat in a wood pile. It was not a pleasant look to be receiving, especially after a night of little sleep and lots of worry.

"Since we're buying it, I thought I'd like to know more about the family who lived there before."

Ruth blinked.

Maggie had an urge to keep talking to fill in the awkward silence that was as uncomfortable as a cramp but she kept her mouth shut, knowing that babbling was only going to make Ruth's gaze sharpen.

The silence stretched uncomfortably to the point where it was another presence in the room. Maggie dug in her heels, however. She was not going to crack. The silence could pull up a chair and have a seat for all she cared. She was not going to speak first.

Ruth blinked at her again from behind her spectacles. "If it's the people you're interested in, you might want to talk to Blue Dixon since he is the owner of the house and the last living Dixon."

"I did," Maggie said. "He recommended that I talk to you."

Ruth considered her for a long moment, and Maggie had a new appreciation for the term *pregnant pause*. She half expected Ruth to have a litter of kittens with the way her face was twitching.

Maggie felt as if Ruth were trying to see way down deep into her soul, and she didn't think she was up for that sort of scrutiny before noon. She had no idea how to convince Ruth to help her. She tried smiling but Ruth just stared unblinking.

"My interest is more in the Dixon house itself," Ruth said. "I don't much care about the family, but the house is one of the original homes in St. Stanley and maintaining it should be a top priority for the owners."

"I agree," Maggie said. She knew Ruth had something

on her mind but she was darned if she could figure it out. She decided her best recourse was to just agree with her.

"What's your plan for it?" Ruth asked.

"I'm not sure I know what you mean," Maggie stalled.

"You're not going to renovate it, are you? You know, knock down walls and change the layout."

"We haven't talked about that, no."

"Because you can't," Ruth said. She crossed her skinny little arms over her chest and narrowed her eyes at Maggie.

"Excuse me?" Maggie felt herself getting irritated.

Maggie had known Ruth Crenshaw her entire life. No, not closely, but in a town the size of St. Stanley everyone knew everyone else even if they rarely spoke to one another.

Ruth was from one of the original families. She prided herself on that. It was undoubtedly why she was the head of the historical society. She even lived in her family's original home, which was coincidentally right down the street from the Dixon house. But perhaps that was why she was concerned that Maggie and Sam planned to change the Dixon house. It would affect her home's value.

Ruth was one of the town eccentrics and was known for being a bit socially defective. At the moment, she was being overly bossy, and Maggie found it was scraping on her last nerve.

"To maintain the historical integrity of the Dixon home, you can't change anything," Ruth said. She bobbed her head while she spoke and Maggie thought she looked like a chicken pecking relentlessly in the dirt. Then she leaned close into Maggie's personal space and her eyes went wide behind her spectacles. "You can't change *anything*."

"Okay," Maggie said.

She was now at the point where it was a matter of pacifying the crazy person. She knew Sam would be in to talk to Ruth later and, although she had agreed to tell Ruth he was coming, now she wasn't so sure. Ruth's obsession with the integrity of their house was making her edgy.

"I have some books that might help you appreciate your new home," Ruth said.

She turned and walked over to one of the bookshelves against the wall. She ran her hand lovingly over the books and pulled three off the shelf. When she held them out to Maggie it was with obvious reluctance.

"You can take these since they are recent histories and we have multiple copies; for anything else you need to come in to use inside the building."

Maggie glanced at the titles. One was about the early families of St. Stanley, another was historic homes and the third was a handbook about the requirements for historical designation for properties in St. Stanley. Subtle, Ruth was not.

"Thanks," Maggie said. "I really appreciate it."

Ruth bobbed her head and Maggie beat a hasty retreat before Ruth changed her mind and snatched the books out of Maggie's hands.

"I'll return these very soon," Maggie said. "I promise."

"I'm sure you will," Ruth said.

Maggie hurried out the door with Ruth still watching her with an intensity that made her skin itch.

As she pushed open the door, she ran into Mary Lou Sutton, who was on her way in.

"Sorry," Maggie said. She dodged to the side to keep from knocking Mary Lou down.

"It's all right," Mary Lou said. She was a sturdy middle-aged woman who wore her short brown hair in a mop of large curls and always had a pair of reading glasses perched on her head. "Don't tell me, let me guess: Ruth is in rare form today."

Maggie smiled in relief. Mary Lou understood.

"A bit," she said.

"I've been here for several months now and every time I walk through the door I wonder if it's a bad day or a good day," Mary Lou said. "Well, at least today I'm prepared. Thanks, Maggie."

"You're welcome," Maggie said. "Good luck."

"Thanks," Mary Lou said. She pulled open the door and called, "Mornin', Ruth."

Maggie hurried down the steps, hopped into her car and drove to her shop. She could feel the pressure of a headache building at the base of her skull. She needed a steaming cup of java and how.

She parked down the street from her shop in a side lot, leaving the spots in front of the store for customers. She took her books and unlocked the front door of her shop, flipping the CLOSED sign to OPEN.

She stored the books and her handbag in the break room and then fired up the coffee pot. She stood beside the pot, tapping her fingers on the counter and staring at it as if that would make it brew any faster.

When she heard the jangle of bells on the front door, she sighed. Then she shook it off. Customers were always a good thing, even precaffeine. She put on her brightest smile and left the break room to greet the person out front.

"Good morning," she said. She glanced across the store to see Mrs. Shoemaker there. A tiny little bird of a woman, Mrs. Shoemaker collected cookie cutters. She had developed a slight hoarding problem when she discovered what all she could buy on eBay, so her children had put her computer on lockdown. Now she came to visit Maggie every week in the hope that Maggie might have some cookie cutters for her.

Maggie was torn between going out of her way to find one or two for the sweet elderly lady just to keep her happy and respecting her family's wishes that she not bury herself alive in cookie cutters. It was a dilemma.

"Good morning, Maggie," Mrs. Shoemaker said. "Get anything new?"

Maggie sighed. She'd been so busy with the house and the wedding—okay, not so much the wedding but definitely the house—that she hadn't thought to put aside anything for Mrs. Shoemaker.

"I'm sorry," she said. "No cookie cutters this week."

"Darn it," Mrs. Shoemaker said. She swung her right fist in an "aw shucks" motion that Maggie found endearing coming from the elderly lady.

"I've just made some coffee," Maggie said. "Would you like a cup?"

"Why, I don't mind if I do." Mrs. Shoemaker beamed.

Maggie gestured for her to sit in the small seating area Maggie kept in the shop. All of the furniture pieces were for sale, so it was an ever-changing arrangement that Maggie felt suited her store's ambiance.

Currently, it was an upholstered loveseat with a matching armchair and a glass coffee table. While Mrs. Shoemaker settled into the armchair Maggie went to fetch the coffee. She used a vintage dish set on a silver tray, all of which were also for sale.

She settled the tray on the table and poured the coffee for Mrs. Shoemaker, letting her add her own milk and sugar. Maggie handed her a cup and then made her own. It was all she could do not to purr when she took the first few sips. It had been a long morning.

Mrs. Shoemaker savored her first few sips as well and then she smiled at Maggie. "The big day is coming soon, isn't it?"

"Just a few more weeks," Maggie agreed.

"You are going to make a lovely bride," Mrs. Shoemaker said.

Maggie looked down into her coffee cup. Bride. She didn't really think of herself that way. To her, a bride seemed like a term for someone who was new to being a grownup. It didn't feel new to her. She did feel like she was on the verge of becoming a wife, and she liked that, but the bride thing. It just didn't feel like it fit quite right.

"Thank you," she said. "We bought the Dixon house, did you hear?"

"I did." Mrs. Shoemaker took a delicate sip of her coffee. "It's about time someone made that old place a home again. I'm so glad it's going to be you and Sam. He's a fine man."

"Thank you. I think so, too."

Maggie glanced at Mrs. Shoemaker. She knew that she had lived in St. Stanley most of her life so it stood to reason that she knew something of the Dixon family history. Maybe she even knew who the skeleton in the root cellar was. It was worth a shot.

"Did you know Ida or Imogene Dixon very well, Mrs. Shoemaker?" Maggie asked.

"Call me Mildred, dear, there's no need for formality between friends," Mrs. Shoemaker said. "No, the Dixon twins were older than me by about ten years. When I was a girl, I thought they were like movie stars. We all watched them from afar."

"All right, Mildred." Maggie smiled. "What do you remember about them?"

"Well, Ida was the dreamer, she always wore pink and loved to recite poetry," Mildred said. "Imogene on the other hand was the practical one. She always looked like she was working out a math problem in her head. She was the caretaker of the two of them. Their mother died when they were teenagers. Imogene stepped up and took over the mother role for Ida, she was the more sensitive one and seemed to suffer from the loss of their mother more. That always made me feel badly for Imogene. She was so busy taking care of Ida that I wondered if anyone ever took care of her."

"Oh, that would have been hard," Maggie agreed. "What about their father?"

"He was a wreck after their mother passed," Mildred said. She paused to sip her coffee. "He tried his best, but really, a man back in the forties had no idea how to raise two teenage girls. It's lucky Imogene was so level-headed."

"Do you know why neither of them ever married?"

"I think Ida was almost married once," Mildred said. "But something happened. It was during the war so he could have been killed and knowing how sensitive Ida was she might not have wanted to marry another."

"And Imogene?"

"She'd never leave Ida," Mildred said. "It's too bad. They were both lookers in their day, with Ida being the more outgoing one while Imogene was rather shy."

"Do you remember who it was that Ida was supposed to marry?" Maggie asked.

Mildred looked thoughtful for a minute and then she shook her head. "No, it was seventy years ago and I'm afraid my brain is too crowded to remember. I'll think on it if you'd like."

"Please," Maggie said.

"Why is it so important?" Mildred asked.

Maggie wondered if she should mention the skeleton in her house. She couldn't even wrap her head around how to start that conversation. She knew it would become public information soon enough but she wasn't sure Sam wanted it known just yet.

"We've found some interesting things in the house," she said. Not a total lie. "So, we're just trying to put together a picture of the Dixon family to get a sense of our new home."

Mildred's gaze was shrewd, as if she knew Maggie wasn't telling her everything.

"Every home is the keeper of the story of the family who has lived there," she said. "When you and Sam move in, you'll be giving it a new story. Don't fret too much about the past, it's over and done and can't be changed."

Maggie nodded. "You're a very wise woman, Mrs. Shoemaker—I mean, Mildred."

"Oh no," Mildred waved a dismissive hand at her. "I've just been around awhile is all. You can't help but pick up a few life lessons along the way."

"I suppose," Maggie agreed.

Mildred glanced at her watch. "Oh dear, I have to go," she said. She put down her cup and rolled out of her seat. "I have an appointment at the Clip and Snip with Eva Martinez. I don't want to be late. She gets insulted if you're not on time, and I don't want her taking it out on my hair."

"Of course. Thanks for visiting with me," Maggie said.

"Oh no, thank you for a lovely time," Mildred said. She paused before pushing open the front door. "A little word of advice, if I may?"

"Absolutely," Maggie said.

"Don't let the ghost scare you off." With that, Mrs. Shoemaker pushed out the door, leaving Maggie slack jawed in her wake.

Ghost! She had said *ghost*! Did Mildred Shoemaker know there was a ghost in the Dixon house? In her and Sam's house?

Maggie was about to call after her, but the door was pulled open again and a handful of customers entered. Darn it!

Chapter 11

Maggie was half tempted to run after her, but then she paused. Wouldn't Mildred have flat-out told her the house was haunted if it was? Maybe she was speaking in the metaphorical sense.

She wanted to call Sam but she hesitated. He was already thumbs-down on her ghost theory and he now had a full plate trying to figure out the identity of their uninvited basement-dwelling houseguest.

Maggie cleaned up after her coffee with Mildred while Marlene Riordan and her daughters Chrissy and Heather shopped for a dining set for Heather's new apartment. Maggie didn't have one at the moment that would fit in Heather's place, but she did have some vintage stemware that Chrissy purchased for her apartment.

When the Riordans left, Patti Simpson and her son Alec popped in, looking for some luggage for his post-college trip to Europe. Maggie just happened to have a set of Lucas bags that had never been used by the previous owner, John Solomon, who had bought the luggage to combat his fear of flying by building excitement for a trip to Fiji. It hadn't worked. Patti and Alec were happy to give the luggage a new home.

Still thinking about what Mildred had told her, Maggie was sorting a box of sweaters donated by Hannah Chisholm. They had the faint smell of moth balls about them, but they were designer sweaters, hand knit of good quality wool. Maggie couldn't do much with them in June but come October they would be a hot ticket.

She was picturing a window display featuring a few of the sweaters when her cell phone rang. The number displayed was Doc Franklin's.

"Hi, Doc," she answered. "Is everything okay?"

"Not exactly," Doc said. "There's been an incident over here at Spring Gardens and Blue Dixon says you can clear it up."

"Incident?" Maggie asked.

"Well, a fight, actually," Doc said.

"Fight? Between who?"

"Blue Dixon and Dennis Applebaum," Doc said. "It got a bit ugly. I've just stitched up Blue's forehead."

"Stitches?" Maggie squeaked. "I'll be right there."

She glanced at her watch. She really could not close in the middle of the day. She wondered if Mrs. Kellerman at the dry cleaner next door would be willing to come over and watch the shop. If she had her assistant in, it should be no problem.

Maggie hurried next door and found Mrs. Kellerman doing some hand tailoring on a blouse. She was more than happy to come and watch Maggie's shop while she ducked out. Maggie promised to return the favor whenever it was needed.

The drive to Spring Gardens was short as it was just across town. Maggie had a horrible image of Blue Dixon with a squashed melon for a head but that was ridiculous as Doc Franklin would have admitted him to the hospital if that were the case. But what could have happened between the two geriatrics that would have caused the poor man to require stitches? And how could Maggie possibly help?

She parked her car and hurried into the office on the side of the building where she had formerly worked as Doc Franklin's bookkeeper. The first person she saw was Cheryl, Doc's number one nurse, and she looked at Maggie with wide eyes as if to say she had never seen anything like this.

"What happened?" Maggie asked.

"Well, hello to you, too," Cheryl said.

"Sorry, hi," Maggie said. She gave the solidly built nurse a quick hug and then stepped back. "But seriously, what happened?"

"Blue took a cane to the forehead," Cheryl said. "While Dennis had his walker knocked out from under him and twisted his ankle."

"Good grief," Maggie said. "Will they be okay?"

"Yeah, just bumps and bruises," Cheryl said. "Doc wanted you to come and talk to them and see if you could clear up the misunderstanding."

"I don't see how I can," Maggie said. "But I'll try."

Cheryl nodded. "They're in examination room three."

"Thanks," Maggie said. She began to stride down the short hallway but Cheryl called her back. "Hey! Tim and I are really looking forward to the wedding! He said Sam said you were serving barbecue. Can I just say, 'Yay!'?"

Maggie gave her a small smile which she hoped covered the dismay that was coursing through her body. Barbecue? When had they decided on barbecue? What could Sam be thinking? Her mother would have a fit and she was pretty sure his mother wasn't going to be doing cartwheels about the menu either.

She rapped lightly on the door to exam room three, waiting just a moment to hear Doc give her the okay before she entered. She pushed the door open cautiously, peering around the edge before she came in. Even peeking first, she was unprepared for the sight that met her eyes.

Doc Franklin was standing between the two gray-haired men, with his arms crossed over his chest, looking as disgusted as Maggie had ever seen him.

"I think you two need to do a nice afternoon of community service after the ruckus you kicked up," Doc Franklin said. "You smashed Mavis Toole's prize orchids in your dustup and you broke Clyde Bushell's favorite chair."

"What? I pay to live here," Dennis Applebaum protested. "I am not doing any manual labor."

Doc Franklin pursed his lips and considered him a moment. "I suppose you could always move out."

"I'm not moving," Dennis blustered.

"Then I suggest you do what I advise and do some community service before the other residents vote you out. There's a waiting list one hundred deep, so it's not like they'll have any trouble replacing you."

"Why do I have to do it?" Dennis whined. "He started it."

Maggie felt her temples contract. She was having a hard time deciding if this guy was seven or seventy. At least now she understood why he wasn't married. Probably, his mother had coddled him all his life and he'd never had to grow up and accept responsibility for his actions.

Judging by the way Doc Franklin's hair was standing on end, his exasperation had peaked. His hair always started the day neatly combed but with each difficult patient it rose to stand straight up until he had his mad scientist look going.

She glanced at Blue Dixon, who had yet to say a word. Instead he was holding an ice pack to his head and looking resigned.

"I'll make the orchid situation right," he said.

"And just what does that leave me with?" Dennis demanded. "The chair? How is that fair?"

Maggie was beginning to understand why Blue had popped him.

"I know about orchids," Blue said. "I can help with those."

"Excellent," Doc said. "And you can split the cost of replacing Clyde's chair."

Blue nodded as if that seemed fair to him.

Dennis looked smug as if he'd gotten away with something until Doc looked at him and added, "And since you don't know anything about orchids, I think you can weed Mavis's ten-by-ten patch in the community garden."

"Aw." Dennis started to complain but Doc cut him off by holding up his hand.

"Enough," Doc said. "Maggie is here to tell you both about the house and put this nonsense to an end."

Maggie glanced at their expectant expressions and she turned to look at Doc in confusion. "What is it exactly that you wanted to know?"

"Is there a ghost in the house?" Blue asked.

She frowned at him. They'd already discussed this.

"Yes, is there?" Dennis asked. "Does it seem malevolent?"

"Huh?" Maggie looked at Doc in confusion.

"Dennis and Blue got into a fistfight because Blue claims the house has a ghost, and Dennis said that if it does it means that clearly one of Blue's relatives must be evil and is haunting the house because they're trapped here and can't move on to the beyond."

"I don't think I'm qualified to speak on this," Maggie said. "You need someone who knows about paranormal stuff. Like spirits and poltergeists and all that jazz."

"You'll do just fine," Blue said. "You've been in the house and felt the presence of an otherworldly being. Since you and Sam bought the house it belongs to you. So, does it feel as if the presence is evil or not?"

Maggie blew out a breath. The presence didn't feel evil but it was definitely there. She didn't care what Sam said.

"No, it's not evil, I think," she said.

"Aha," Blue snapped at Dennis. "There you have it. Not evil."

"But she said 'I think,'" Dennis insisted. "She doesn't know. It only figures that it's evil and someone in your family caused it or maybe it's Ida or Imogene. They never did marry and they lived in that house for a mighty long time by themselves. Maybe they were witches."

Blue struggled to get to his feet. He had his hands balled into fists and a fire in his eye when he bellowed, "Why you . . . I'll knock your head off for that."

"Whoa, whoa, whoa," Doc Franklin said as he pushed Blue back down into a seated position. "Settle down there, Blue, there is absolutely no fighting in my office and you know it."

"But he's slandering my family," Blue protested. "I can't have that. I lost three dates for next week because of him. If this keeps up, I may have to learn to cook for myself."

"It might do you some good," Doc Franklin said.

"Don't even joke," Blue said.

"I'm just stating the facts," Dennis protested. "I can't help it if the ladies are afraid of you now that they know you have bad kin in your family. You can't blame the ladies. If it's genetic, they have to be worried for their safety with you. Who knows when you might snap."

"What? I'd never hurt a lady, and I do not have bad kin," Blue protested. "No one in the Dixon family is a killer."

"That's right," Maggie said. "Just because we found a skeleton . . ."

She caught herself too late. All three men turned to stare at her in surprise and Maggie knew there was no taking back what she had just said. Oops.

Chapter 12

"What skeleton?" Doc Franklin asked.

"Um," Maggie stalled.

"Skeleton?" Dennis lit up like a firecracker. "Ha, I knew it. There's a murderer in your past, Blue Dixon."

"There is not!" Blue shouted. His face was a mottled red.

"This wasn't exactly what I was hoping for when I sent for you," Doc Franklin said to Maggie.

She bit her lip. "Sorry."

"Not your fault," he said. "A skeleton?"

"Yes, in uniform," Maggie said. "It seems he has been there for a very long time. Sam is trying to identify him as we speak."

"Just wait 'til I tell the ladies about the skeleton in

your closet. Get it?" Dennis chortled. "We'll see who is getting the home-cooked hot dishes then, won't we?"

"Why you . . . that's it. I'm going to punch you right in the mouth," Blue said.

Dennis put up his fists, looking like he was ready to go. Doc Franklin stepped in and held up his hands, stopping the two of them from getting anywhere near each other. He frowned at the men on either side of him.

"Why do I get the feeling that this is more about casseroles than it is about the Dixon house being haunted or not?" he asked.

Dennis's eyebrows lowered and his upper lip curled. "It's his fault."

Blue raised his hands in exasperation. "What is my fault? You start bad-mouthing me to all of the ladies, saying that there are evil ghosts in my family home and that I am likely to go crazy and kill people and that's my fault?"

"Me and my brother had it pretty good with the ladies before you got here," Dennis said. "They took good care of us with Sunday dinner invites and doing our laundry. Then this clown shows up with his pretty manners and suave suits and my brother and I have had to learn how to do our own laundry and we haven't had anyone drop off a meal in months."

"Maybe it's because you two have the manners of barnyard animals," Blue said. "Sylvia Perch told me that you just dumped your laundry on her doorstep like she was your maid."

"She liked doing it," Dennis protested.

"Really?" Maggie asked. The feminist within her was having a conniption. "You actually think she *wanted* to launder your shorts?"

She said it in a tone that made it clear she thought he was as dense as a cinder block. Dennis's cheeks turned a vibrant shade of red, and she knew she'd made her point. Dennis wasn't one to stop digging himself into a hole once he'd begun shoveling, however, so he started to protest.

"Well, she was perfectly happy to do my laundry until he showed up and started giving all the ladies flowers and candy and taking them to movies," he said. He glared at Blue. "You ruined everything."

"I'd say it's more like I liberated those poor ladies, if you ask me," Blue said. "If a woman does something nice for you, you should do a kindness in turn or at the very least let her know you appreciate it. Good god, man, everyone knows you're rich. Why don't you use some of your wealth to spread some joy to the ladies? Then you'd be in the running again as they'd likely overlook your abysmal manners. You should try to evolve a few steps beyond knuckle-dragging cave dweller."

Dennis started to growl, so Doc Franklin stepped in between them again.

"Seems to me you fellas need to find a compromise," Doc said. "How about if Blue schools you in the art of winning over the ladies?"

"What?" Dennis and Blue cried together. They looked equally appalled at the idea of spending any time together.

Doc continued, "The ladies like Blue because he treats

them well, you want the ladies to like you, Dennis, so it seems to me the only solution is to get Blue to teach you how to woo the ladies. And Blue, there are far too many ladies for you to manage on your own, so it shouldn't be a hardship to share."

Dennis looked at Blue suspiciously. "My brother, too."

"Great," Blue muttered. "Now I have the Applebaum brothers for an entourage."

"Well?" Doc asked.

"No more cracks about my family," Blue said. He gave Dennis a dark look.

"Deal," Dennis said. He held out his hand and Blue shook it. "But you have to admit a skeleton in the house could be good material."

Blue considered him for a moment and then turned to Maggie with a confused look. "I've been in that house a few times to check on things, and I've never seen a skeleton. Where did you find it?"

"It was in the basement in a root cellar that had been blocked off by a shelf full of canning jars," she said. "We never would have found it but the light went out and Sam and I went down to check the circuit breaker. While we were checking it out, I found the door to the cellar and there he was."

"How do you know it was a he?" Doc asked.

"The uniform," Maggie said. "It was military with pilot's wings, but the section where the name would be had rotted away. We're thinking he may have been a soldier in World War Two."

Doc Franklin's eyes went wide at this, and Maggie

knew that he had been just a kid during the Second World War.

"I don't suppose you remember anyone going missing around then?" she asked.

Doc ran a hand through his white hair. "Killed in battle, sure, but missing, no."

Maggie nodded her head. She'd figured if it was someone local there'd have been a story about him. No, whoever this guy was he had to have been someone who was passing through.

She glanced at Blue. "How about you? Do you remember any soldiers in the family or that were friends of the family?"

Blue looked thoughtful and shook his head. "I really didn't know my cousins that well during the war. They were several years older than me and I was just a kid back then. We didn't get close until I was a teenager."

Maggie looked at Dennis and he shrugged. "We didn't live here then. My family was in Dumontville, working in the factories."

"It was a long time ago," Maggie said. "Sam is bringing in someone from the Richmond PD to help him, an old pal of his named Andy. I hope he can give us something to go on."

"Do you think the skeleton is the presence in the house?" Blue asked. He sounded equal parts thrilled and nervous. Yeah, sure, because the house wasn't his problem anymore.

"No idea," Maggie said. "Sam insists that there is no ghost. He thinks it's just drafty."

"But you don't agree?" Doc Franklin asked.

"I don't know," Maggie said. "One minute I think one thing and the next I think something else entirely. You're a man of science, what do you think? Are ghosts real?"

Doc tapped his finger against his lips. Maggie knew this was a stalling tactic of his that he employed when a patient was pushing for a diagnosis and he wasn't ready to render an opinion.

"The world is full of the unexplained," he said.

"Oh, boo hiss," Dennis said. "That's no answer."

"Maybe not, but unless either of you gentlemen is in pain or still bleeding, I believe our time together is done."

Doc pulled the curtain between their two beds, giving them privacy to dress. He then gestured for Maggie to follow him and led the way out of exam room three.

"Thank you for coming by," Doc said. "I wasn't having much luck sorting that mess until you showed up."

"I can't believe they were fighting over the ladies," Maggie said. "That's crazy."

"Not to a lonely old man it isn't," Doc said.

"So, how are you and Alice doing?" Maggie asked.

Doc beamed at her and that was all the answer Maggie needed. "She's been teaching Bianca how to make pie."

Maggie's eyebrows shot up on her forehead. Bianca was Doc's grown daughter from a prior assignation. Alice had always wanted children but had been unable to have any. When she found out about Doc's daughter with another woman, the betrayal had run deep, even though Doc himself hadn't known. For Alice to be reaching out to Bianca was huge.

"That's great, Doc," Maggie said.

He nodded and looked a little emotional when he continued, "Alice is thinking that if Bianca and her fiancé Max have children she will get to be a grandmother, and goodness knows, she'd make a terrific one."

"Are you kidding?" Maggie asked. "She'd be amazing and since neither Bianca nor Max have any real family, well, it does seem right, doesn't it?"

"Yes, it does," Doc agreed. Again, he looked a bit emotional so Maggie gave him a quick fierce hug. When she stepped back, he said, "But enough about us, what about you and Sam? The big day is coming and I hear you two are planning to get hitched in the middle of the town square with Tim Kelly manning the bar. Is that true?"

"The town green with a bar?" Maggie asked. "This is the first I'm hearing of it. Sheesh, Doc, I don't even have my dress yet."

"Well, don't you think you'd better get on that?" he asked. "Time's a-wasting and you and Sam have a lot of years to make up for."

"Yeah," she said. "I am on it. We will get it together. You'll see. It'll be amazing."

Doc grinned. "I never doubted it for a second."

Maggie left with a wave and a case of nerves that felt like bats swooping around in her belly. What was she going to do? The wedding was just weeks away. She had done nothing. Her house was haunted. There was a skeleton in her basement. And she was pretty sure she was developing a rash.

She itched the skin at her elbow as she climbed back

into her car. Everything was going to be fine. They'd figure out who the skeleton was, the ghost would leave, and the wedding would fall into place just as it should. No worries.

She drove back through St. Stanley, pondering all that had happened over the past few days. She'd bought her dream house. Yay. Her house was haunted. Boo. She was marrying the man of her dreams. Yay. She hadn't done a thing to plan the wedding. Boo.

Well, at least things seemed to be very balanced. She couldn't argue with the distribution of good and bad but she sure wished the timing were different.

At the stop sign she pulled out her phone to check and see if there was a voice message from Sam. She always kept the volume off on her phone, since she didn't like to hear messages coming in as she then felt compelled to answer them, which would be awkward when she was with a customer. No, it was much easier to wait until she had a minute and then listen to them all at once.

There was no voice mail from Sam nor was there a text message. She put her phone away and continued driving through town. Near the police station she instinctively glanced at the squat redbrick building to see if she could get a glimpse of her man. Sam-watching, sort of like bird-watching, was her new favorite hobby.

She saw his familiar head of dark brown hair and looked more closely to confirm that it was him striding up the walkway toward the station. He wasn't alone. She assumed that his friend from the Richmond PD was the person in the official-looking slacks and dress shirt walking beside him. Somehow she had not expected the man she had pictured as Andy to have curves like that.

As Maggie watched, Andy tossed her long, glossy black hair over her shoulder and tipped her head back to show a delicate profile and a flawless smile as she laughed at something Sam said. Hmm.

Maggie felt her right front tire skim the curb and she jerked the wheel to the left to keep from running off the road. She continued on to her shop, mulling over this alarming turn of events in her mind. To her credit she only glanced over her shoulder back at Sam and company twice—okay, three times but really that was it.

Chapter 13

Maggie thanked Mrs. Kellerman for her help and went to make a fresh pot of coffee. She had a feeling she was going to need it to get through the afternoon.

She had sent Sam a text asking about his friend Andy's arrival and Sam had texted back that *she* had just gotten to town and he was taking her over to the house to inspect the scene.

Okaaaaaay, then. Maggie assured herself that she was okay with it. Completely 100% okay with the man she'd pictured in her head actually being a gorgeous woman. Yup, nothing to worry about here.

She was just taking her first bracing sip of coffee and repeating her "no worries" mantra when the front door opened and Joanne came in with baby Patience strapped to her chest in one of those complicated wrap things that Maggie was quite glad was not in vogue when she'd had her daughter. One glance at the baby and she could feel her skin getting sweaty and sticky.

Although, she had to admit Patience looked to be the picture of contentment snuggled close to her mama. Maggie was hit with a pang of guilt. Had she damaged Laura and given her abandonment issues by not lashing her to her chest during her baby years? She shook her head. What was she thinking? Laura was a bright and beautiful confident young woman on an internship in New York City. She was totally fine. Apparently, mother's guilt had no expiration date. Awesome.

"Okay, so Michael called me and told me that Pete told him that Sam told him that the two of you found a skeleton in your house last night. True?"

Maggie hadn't thought Sam would let the story out so early. Then again, given how gossip moved at the speed of sound in St. Stanley, she was surprised it had taken this long for someone to come in and ask about it.

"True," she said.

Joanne gasped and clapped a hand over her mouth. Baby Patience stirred and Joanne cringed and began to rock from foot to foot in a soothing "rock-a-bye baby" motion. Once Patience settled, she looked up at Maggie.

"Details," she whispered.

"There isn't much," Maggie said, keeping her voice soft. "We found it in the basement in a blocked-off root cellar, but we don't know who it is—er, was. The clothes, well, the uniform looks to be from the forties."

"This is unbelievable," Joanne breathed.

The door opened again but this time it was Ginger. She was wearing one of her favorite broomstick skirts with the sparkles on the bottom. She saw Joanne rocking back and forth and gently closed the door behind her.

"Explain," she hissed at Maggie.

There was no need to ask what Ginger was referring to, so Maggie told her the same thing that she had told Joanne. Ginger's eyes went wide and she looked nervous.

"So there is a ghost in the Dixon house. Oh my god, in your house!"

"I think so," Maggie said.

"Sam doesn't?" Joanne asked.

"No, he is certain that all the banging doors, lights flickering and drafty breezes were just the house settling or the wind," Maggie said.

"Even after finding the body?" Ginger asked.

"Skeleton," Maggie corrected her. "There was no body, just bones."

She gave an involuntary shudder and her friends did as well.

"What are you going to do?" Ginger asked. "What if the poor man was murdered there? You can't live in a house where there was a murder."

"I know," Maggie said. "But both Sam and I think that if we can figure out what happened, we'll feel better about it. I mean maybe there is a perfectly logical explanation for all of this."

The door opened again and in strode Claire. She was

dressed for work at the library in a black skirt, green blouse and black pumps.

"I only have a few minutes until my break is over," she said. "I have to be on the reference desk in fifteen minutes, so start talking."

She glanced at her wristwatch and then at Maggie. Taking the hint, Maggie gave her the short version of the events of the past evening.

"I think Sam is right," Claire said. She pushed her rectangular glasses up on her nose. "You may find that the poor man died of natural causes, which would make the house perfectly fine to live in."

"Yeah, except for the moaning, door slamming and random lights going out," Ginger said. "I say sell it, no matter what. Better yet, march over to Marcy Hayes's office and tear that contract up right in her face."

Maggie had thought about doing just that but with her luck, Marcy would have her arrested by her own fiancé. That was a thought too embarrassing to contemplate.

When the door opened again, Maggie was relieved. With all of the Good Buy Girls here it had to be a customer. She put on her best smile and turned to face the door. Her smile fell faster than a brick off a tall building when she realized who was standing in her shop, looking like she owned the place.

"What?" Summer asked. "Can't a gal be neighborly?"

Yeah, the last time Summer had tried to be neighborly, she'd been pushed by her mother to try and steal Sam away from Maggie with every trick in the book, including having Maggie walk in on them in a seedy motel on the outskirts of town. Since Summer had married Tyler Fawkes, she had seemed to turn over a new leaf, but still, a lifetime of enmity was a hard thing to shake off.

"What can I do for you, Summer?" Maggie asked. She was pleased that her voice came out cordial instead of filled with hostility and suspicion.

Summer tossed her long blond hair over her shoulder and smoothed the front of her sundress. Marriage had also toned down Summer's usual woman-on-the-prowl look a notch or two and it occurred to Maggie that if she was meeting Summer for the first time she wouldn't consider her a she-devil. At least not right away.

"It's not what you can do for me, but what I can do for you," Summer said.

Maggie gave her a sideways look and noticed that Ginger, Joanne and Claire were doing the same.

"How do you figure?" Maggie asked.

"I saw that woman with Sam," Summer said. "She's trouble."

"No, she isn't," Maggie said.

"Excuse me?" Summer gaped. "Did you *see* her?"

"Yes, I did," Maggie said. "So what?"

She knew she sounded defensive but she couldn't help it. Summer was putting voice to her own worries about Andy and she didn't like it.

"What woman with Sam?" Ginger asked Maggie with one hand on her hip as if she was all put out that Maggie had been withholding information.

"Andy Lowenstein," Maggie said. "She's a colleague of Sam's from the Richmond PD. She's in forensics and is here to help identify the skeleton."

"And she's hot," Summer said. "And young. Young and hot is not your friend, especially when he has yet to put a ring on it."

"Gee, thanks for coming in today, Summer," Maggie said. "As usual you're doing wonders for my self-esteem."

"Oh, don't be like that," Summer said. "I'm here to help."

"Please," Claire said.

"Honestly," Joanne added.

"Do we look that dumb?" Ginger asked.

"No, I'm serious," Summer said. "Running off competing women is a particular gift of mine."

"She does have a knack," Joanne conceded.

"But why would you want to help me? If we can twist this situation enough to think that running a forensic investigator off of an assignment is helpful, that is," Maggie said.

Summer studied the pretty coral-colored polish on her fingernails. She seemed embarrassed and Maggie wondered what could make the blonde bombshell look so self-conscious.

"Tyler, well, he has a lot of friends," Summer said.

"It's true," Ginger said. "He's always the first one to help when someone needs a hand and he has a great sense of humor."

"He was a dear helping us get the baby's furniture into

the nursery," Joanne said. "I don't know what we would have done without him."

"And he always helps out at the annual book sale for the library. He dresses up in our dragon costume and dances on the corner drawing people into the sale. The kids love him," Claire added. "He's a huge Frank Herbert fan."

"That's an author, right?" Summer asked.

Claire nodded. To her credit, she didn't make a "duh" face.

"What does Tyler being well liked have to do with you being here now?" Maggie asked.

"Because Tyler is popular and has loads of friends, and I . . . I don't have any," Summer wailed.

She lowered her head and sobbed into her open hands. If Maggie hadn't already been having the weirdest week of her life, this moment surely would have taken the blue ribbon for bizarre. Summer in her shop, sobbing, looking for friends: It just didn't get any more odd.

Ginger and the others looked at her and Maggie realized that since she and Summer had been enemies, oh, since they'd first spied each other in pigtails and kneesocks, they were waiting for her to give a sign as to what to do.

Maggie studied Summer and a sigh welled up inside of her. She would have to have a shriveled-up prune for a heart to ignore the big gushing sobs that were wracking Summer's busty frame.

"There, there," she said. She snatched a tissue out of the box nearby and handed it to Summer. "Don't cry."

Ginger raised her eyebrows, giving Maggie the signal that she sounded about as sincere as a sinner with a hangover on Sunday.

Maggie rolled her eyes and Ginger made a shooing gesture with her hands in Summer's direction. Maggie would have stomped her foot in protest but she didn't want to wake the baby.

She stepped forward and looped an arm around Summer's shoulders. Summer lifted her head and used the tissue Maggie gave her to dab at her eyes. She had the big raccoon mascara circles going, so at least her tears had been genuine.

"How can I not cry?" Summer asked. "Tyler is everything that is good and I'm, well, I'm just a horrible person."

"No one is all bad," Claire said. She looked sympathetic and Maggie knew it was because of her own checkered past. "Everyone has their good points."

Maggie frantically scanned her brain trying to come up with Summer's good points. She was drawing a blank. She was sure if she was a man, she could have started with her knockout figure and ended with her propensity for dressing like a slut, but she wasn't a dude and she and Summer had been enemies for a very long time.

"Yeah, I'm sure you have many fine qualities," Joanne agreed. Maggie didn't think she was the only one who heard the lack of conviction in Joanne's voice.

"Do you mean it?" Summer asked.

She looked so vulnerable that all of Maggie's friends moved forward as one to pat her on the back and give her a kind word of encouragement. Even Maggie found herself muttering something that sounded, well, not like an insult, so that was encouraging.

"So, you mean it?" Summer asked. Her face lit up and she clapped her hands together. "I'm in?"

"In what?" Maggie asked suspiciously.

"Your group, stu . . . er . . . silly," Summer said with a grin. "I'm a Good Buy Girl."

Chapter 14

Maggie felt her chest constrict like she was a diver with decompression sickness, aka the bends. She could not have heard what she thought she heard. Could she? She put her finger in her ear to make sure a wax ball wasn't impairing her hearing.

"Repeat that again," Maggie said.

Summer leaned close and spoke loudly in Maggie's ear. "I'm a Good Buy Girl."

Maggie glanced at the others. They looked as flummoxed as she felt and the baby was beginning to fuss. She mouthed the words *Help me* to the others but they all glanced away. Clearly, no one was up for another bout of Summer's tears.

The baby began to wail and Joanne looked overjoyed. "Oh dear, time to feed the baby. Excuse me."

She hustled out of the shop with Claire right behind her, exclaiming, "Look at the time. My break is definitely over, way over, in fact, I'm sure I'm late for the desk."

Ginger tried to sidle to the door but Maggie locked her fingers around Ginger's wrist in a grip that would require a sharp blade to be severed.

"Where are you going?" Maggie asked.

"Client?" Ginger guessed.

"No," Maggie said.

"Okay," Ginger sighed.

"Come on, guys, it'll be great," Summer said. "We can shop together and have coffee at the Daily Grind."

"Yeah, here's the problem," Maggie said. "The Good Buy Girls look out for one another. We share sale and bargain information and clip coupons together. It's a more cooperative relationship, which we all know is not really your forte."

"What does that mean?" Summer asked. She looked truly perplexed.

"Sharing is not your gift," Ginger said.

"Oh, I know," Summer said. "I'll work on it. I don't like sharing my clothes, jewelry or men, but I can share other things."

"Such as?" Maggie asked.

"Knowledge," Summer said.

Maggie and Ginger exchanged a glance.

"Explain," Maggie said.

"This Andy woman is not just here to help Sam with

a case," Summer said. "She's working an angle. I saw them together at the Daily Grind and I heard them—"

"Wait, they were at the coffee shop?" Ginger clarified.

"Oh yeah, and she was talking about this old case they'd worked on together and that old case they'd solved together," Summer said. "It was a regular jog down memory lane for the two of them."

Maggie felt a sludgy icky twist in her insides. She was not a jealous person, generally speaking, as she had realized long ago, thanks to Summer, that it was a largely useless emotion. But she had just gotten Sam back in her life and there was a huge chunk of time that they had been apart, and while she loved him and felt like she knew him, she clearly didn't know every single detail of the twenty years they'd spent apart and Andy seemed like she might be a big detail.

"Now listen," Summer said. "I can advise you on how to handle this."

Maggie was tempted, oh, was she tempted, to take Summer up on her offer. She let go of Ginger and took up her coffee mug. She took a long bracing sip.

"Thanks for the offer, Summer," she said. "But I'm okay."

"Oh, good grief," Summer said with a shake of her blond hair. "You're not going to listen to me, are you?"

"I trust Sam," Maggie said.

"You are an idiot," Summer said.

"Hey!" Maggie snapped.

"Now, now ladies, let's keep it cordial." Ginger stepped in between them. "There's no need to lose our tempers."

She gave Maggie a pointed look and Maggie turned away. She was not going to be lectured about how to talk to Summer.

"You're right," Summer said. She shook her hair out and forced a smile. "There, I've forgiven you already."

"You've forgiven me?" Maggie sputtered. "I don't need your—"

"I don't know why I get so upset," Summer interrupted. "It's just a misunderstanding."

"No, it's not," Maggie protested. "You and I have nothing in common. Friendships have to have common ground. We have nothing."

"Not true," Summer said. She stepped away from the counter and began to look through Maggie's shop. "We were both born and raised here in St. Stanley."

"That's a circumstance of geography," Maggie argued. She heard a funny sound coming from Ginger and when she glanced at her she was pretty sure Ginger was trying not to laugh.

"We both own secondhand stores," Summer said.

Maggie wanted to point out that it was because Summer had copied her but she refrained. Instead, she stated the obvious, "Which makes us each other's competition thus not friends."

"We've both been in love with Sam Collins," Summer said. Then she glanced at Maggie and grinned. "That's three for three."

"I'm not going to be able to get rid of you, am I?" Maggie asked. It was beginning to sink into her head that she was not going to be able to talk Summer out of this madness.

"No, you're not," Summer said. "I'm telling you, Mrs. Tyler Fawkes is a brand-new person, a better person. You'll want me as a friend. You'll see."

With a swish of her long blond hair, she left the shop, leaving Maggie and Ginger gaping after her.

"Because I don't have enough on my plate with a wedding to plan, a skeleton in my house, my mother in town and Andy being a good-looking woman instead of the beer-bellied, hairy-eared man I thought she was, I now have this?" Maggie asked.

Ginger nodded. "So it would seem."

"Summer as a friend," Maggie said. "It's like quantum physics. I can't even wrap my brain around the concept for more than a second before poof! It goes away."

"Maybe it's just a phase that will pass," Ginger said.

"Like the moon?" Maggie asked.

"Don't werewolves come out at the full moon? What phase is it in right now?"

"I think it's full," Maggie said. "So, Summer wanting to be our friend is like being stalked by a werewolf?"

"There are marked similarities," Ginger said.

"I don't know. She wasn't looking very hairy."

"That's a myth."

"So, werewolves aren't hairy?"

"That one isn't at any rate."

"So, we like Summer as a werewolf more than we like the idea of her genuinely wanting to be our friend?" Maggie asked.

"Yup," Ginger agreed, making a popping sound on the *P*.

"Okay, then," Maggie said.

Ginger pulled Maggie in for a bracing hug. "Don't fret. Everything is going to be just fine."

"The wedding—" Maggie began but Ginger interrupted.

"Will be beautiful."

"The skeleton—"

"Will be identified. As if you even need it to be, knowing you and Sam you've probably already named it."

"Captain Bones," Maggie said.

"See?"

"Andy the hottie who was supposed to be a man—"

"Will go back to Richmond sad and alone," Ginger said.

Maggie let out a pent-up breath and felt her shoulders drop. "Thanks. I needed that."

Her cell phone chimed from its holder on the counter. Maggie glanced at the display and frowned. "My mother."

"On that note, I am out of here," Ginger said. She blew Maggie a kiss from the door. "Good luck."

She waved and tried not to have pouty voice when she answered the phone.

"Hi, Mom," she answered.

"Sweetie, where are you?"

"At the shop," she said.

"Excellent, I'll be right there," her mother said.

"Why? Is something wrong?" Maggie asked. Her first thought was for her daughter Laura and her second was her grand-nephew Josh. Had something happened to one of them?

"I'll say," her mother said. Her tone sounded irritated instead of alarmed, which should have been Maggie's first clue. "We need to talk."

"What about?"

"Your future mother-in-law," her mother said. "I ran into her at the florist and she was actually picking your floral arrangements."

"What?"

"I know," her mother continued. "Can you imagine? Does she have no sense of propriety or boundaries? I am not certain what sort of family you are marrying into, Maggie."

"Mom, you've known the Collins family for decades," Maggie said. "They're a lovely family as you've said yourself."

"Be that as it may, she was picking your flowers," her mother said.

Maggie was quiet for a moment. "Um, so what were you doing at the florist, Mom?"

"I, well, I was merely pricing them for you, you know, for your bouquet and boutonnieres," she said.

"Oh, and what were you thinking for my bouquet?" Maggie asked.

"Well, I thought an armful of Gerber daisies would be colorful but she was picking out lavender roses," her mother complained and followed it up with a retching noise.

Maggie rubbed her temples with the fingers of her available hand. She inhaled through her nose, held it and slowly exhaled. Everything was going to be fine.

She and Sam were getting married. Everything else was just details.

"Hey, I'm pulling up in front of the shop," her mother said. "Now about your dress, I had some ideas . . ."

Her mother kept talking but Maggie slowly lowered her phone to the counter. All she could think when she reviewed the insanity of her day was, What next?

Chapter 15

She shouldn't have asked. Maggie listened to her mother rattle on about her plans for the wedding. How they were supposed to pull off what her mother wanted to be the social event of the season in less than three weeks Maggie had no idea.

When her mother finally exited the shop, Maggie sagged against the counter in relief. Her anxiety was spiking and she was pretty sure the only cure would be to down an entire bottle of wine. Somehow, she didn't think that would go over too well the next morning, but it was still oh so tempting.

Since there seemed to be a lull in customers, Maggie decided it was as good a time as any to crack open the books Ruth had lent her and study up on the Dixons.

Surely, given that they were one of the older families in St. Stanley, if there was any gossip, it would be chronicled in the books.

She started with the prominent families of St. Stanley book. It showed the most promise, with an entire chapter devoted to the Dixons.

Neil Dixon arrived in St. Stanley when it was just a tiny crossroads, a small farming town in southern Virginia.

Maggie wondered what Neil would think of it if he could see it now. It wasn't much bigger than that long-ago crossroads, but they did have a town green, schools and a small hospital. St. Stanley had gone through wars, depressions, recessions, and it was still here. She thought Neil would approve.

The text was dry, written by a local historian who, while well meaning, had prose that was overblown and flouncy and as dry as dirt. She always thought fiction writers would be the best ones to write history textbooks for the very reason that they could make them come to life.

She plodded through several generations, relieved when she finally got to names that she knew. There was mention of when the house was built, long before the Civil War, but mostly the chapter was about the people who made up the Dixon clan.

There was a long line of inventors and scientists, followed by local politicians; a Dixon had been the town mayor back in the early nineteen-hundreds. Post–Depression era Dixons were more involved in economics and banking, clearly not trusting their money to any unknown institutions ever again. Ida and Imogene Dixon made up the last chapter. At the time the book was published, both sisters were still alive and residing on their own in the family estate.

Ida Dixon was the more creative of the twins. She loved theater and painting, and her family supported her interests in the arts. Imogene was the more pragmatic of the two and preferred a good book to the company of people. Maggie thought the author sounded as if he were writing from personal experience and she wondered if Imogene had rebuffed queries for an interview.

Apparently, Imogene had been very civic-minded and had overseen the library as well as the historical society at one time. Maggie had only known the sisters in their later years and only from a distance. Ida had always dressed feminine in big floppy sun hats with gloves and flouncy dresses. Imogene, on the other hand, wore tailored slacks with crisp blouses. Maggie had always gotten the feeling that Imogene could have been the CEO of a major company with her snappy duds and sharp mind and, now that she was learning more about her, she knew her impression had been correct.

The book made no mention of either sister ever marrying or having children. The author mentioned one poignant moment during his interview with Ida, who was seventy-five at the time, when her eyes grew misty and she glanced away when asked why she had never married. After she composed herself, she said, "My one true love found another more to his liking and left me to pine. I never found another quite like him and so I stayed alone."

Maggie felt her throat get tight at the thought of a woman missing out on her one true love and spending her days longing for him. She closed the book and glanced up to find Sam smiling at her.

"Ah!" she cried. Then she put her hand over her heart. "Give a girl a little warning, why don't you?"

The crinkles around Sam's eyes deepened. "The bells jangled, I coughed, I called your name, and you heard none of it."

"I was engrossed," Maggie said.

"So I gathered," he said. "I'm glad I wasn't a burglar here to rob you. You'd have been cleaned out before you noticed. So what lurid story are you reading?"

"The history of the Dixon family," she said. She came around the counter and hugged him tight. "Poor Ida, she said she pined all her days for the love of her life, who left her for another. It was just so sad."

Sam hugged her in return. A really good one that melded her to his solid frame and made her feel safe and secure. Then he sealed it by kissing the top of her head.

"Good thing you never have to worry about that," he said. "We'll be married in a few weeks and then you'll never be able to shake me loose."

"Promise?" she asked.

"Promise," he said.

Maggie glanced around the shop. There were no surprise customers or family members. It was just the two of them.

"So, where's your friend?" she asked. "Andy?"

"She's out at the house, checking over the scene," he said. "I'll introduce you later."

"Great," Maggie said. "Funny thing about the name Andy, I thought it was a man's."

"Oh." Sam looked surprised. "Didn't I mention that she's a she?"

"Nope," she said.

"Am I in trouble?" he asked.

Maggie laughed. "Not with me but you might want to duck if you see Summer Fawkes coming your way."

Sam stepped back and cocked his head like a dog hearing the fire truck coming through the neighborhood.

"Do tell," he said. It wasn't a request so much as an order.

Maggie told him all about Summer's visit, her desire to be a Good Buy Girl and her suspicions about Andy. When she was finished, Sam was quiet for a moment but then a chuckle busted out of him, and he shook his head.

"Well, I can honestly say I never saw that coming," he said.

"Me either," she agreed. "But just for clarity's sake, which part did you find the most amusing? Summer wanting to be my friend or Summer thinking Andy is warm for your form."

"Both, but probably Summer wanting to be your friend is the big shocker," Sam said. "But just so you don't have any misgivings, let me tell you right now that Andy isn't my type, but even more telling, I'm not hers. Andy likes girls."

"Oh . . . oh!" Maggie said. "I like her already."

"I thought you might," he said. "So, how about we head over to the house and you can meet her and see what a genius she is with old bones?"

Maggie glanced around the shop. There really wasn't any reason to stay open for another half hour until closing.

"Sounds like a plan," she said. "I'll go get my things. We do need to talk."

"What?" he protested. "I thought I cleared it up with the whole 'she doesn't play with boys' speech."

Maggie grabbed the rest of the books and her purse from the back room and joined him by the counter. She liked Sam when he was flustered. He looked anxious like a boy who broke a window with a slingshot and was trying to do the right thing and not run off even though his feet were itching to fly.

"No, it's not about Andy," she said. "It's worse."

Now he looked concerned. "How much worse?"

"Our mothers," she said.

"Oh." He visibly sagged and Maggie had a feeling he'd been on the receiving end of his own mother's lectures.

"They 'bumped' into each other at the florist's while they were each trying to pick our flowers for us," she said.

"Was there bloodshed? Do I have to put out a warrant for their arrests?"

He pushed off of the counter and dropped his arm over her shoulders while they walked to the door.

"Not that I'm aware of but I think it's clear they did not see eye to eye on the floral arrangements."

"Correct me if I'm wrong, but shouldn't you be picking those out?"

He let go of Maggie and opened the door. He waited while she locked it and then pulled her close again as they strode up the sidewalk to his car.

"Yes, but I'm feeling very indecisive," she said. "I can't seem to pick a venue, a dress, flowers, food. I don't mean to have a mental meltdown, but there is no way we are ready to get married in a few weeks."

"Sure we are," he said.

Maggie looked at him as if he was crazy.

"Darling, the only thing we need to get married is you, me, a marriage license and Pastor Shields," he said. "I'm pretty sure I have a lock on you and me, the license is good to go and Pastor Shields has us booked. Everything else is just details."

Maggie stopped walking and turned to look at him. "You really mean that, don't you?"

"Maggie O'Brien Gerber, I have loved you since I first laid eyes on you in preschool. It's taken me forty years to get you to love me, too, and I am not about to let flowers, mothers or any other nonsense jam up the most important day of my life. Am I clear?"

Maggie threw her arms around his neck and kissed him hard on the mouth. She did love it when he used his sheriff voice on her. As always, the attraction between them turned what should have been a quick kiss into one that was smoking hot, and when Dale Mercer drove by, he felt compelled to hold the horn on his truck down for a nice long blast and shout a suggestion that they get a room.

Maggie and Sam broke apart and while Maggie felt her face heat up in embarrassment, Sam looked overly pleased with himself. She was pretty sure he swaggered all the way to his waiting car.

He opened the door for her and she paused before climbing in to study his handsome face. Sometimes it tripped her up how much she loved him, how giddy he made her feel, how unexpected these feelings were in her forties. She was so grateful for this second chance with the first man she'd ever loved.

"For the record," she said. "It didn't take me forty years to fall in love with you. I've loved you, too, ever since we tussled in preschool."

This time when Sam kissed her, it was a soul-deep connection of complete understanding.

Maggie was a bit taken aback by the number of cars in the driveway to their house. Most were official-looking vehicles but some were personal cars. She assumed they belonged to people who wanted to get a look-see at the skeleton in their root cellar. Sam was forced to park on the street in front of their house instead of in the drive.

"How many people are in our house?" she asked. They walked single file passed the cars in the driveway.

"It varies from hour to hour," he said. "But only the important people have access to the basement."

They stepped up onto the porch to find Deputy Dot Wilson and Deputy Stephen Rourke playing cards while sitting on the front steps.

As soon as he saw Sam, Deputy Rourke rose to his feet but Dot stayed put. She was not a pushover for the boss like the younger officers were.

"I do not have any threes. Go Fish," she said. She glanced at Sam and Maggie over her cards. "I heard from Sally Richmond at the grocery who heard from Rene Zucker at the hospital that there is supposed to be a bacon station at your reception. Is that true?"

Maggie and Sam exchanged surprised glances. Maggie shrugged and Sam shrugged in return.

"I thought so," Dot said with a huff. "Well, just so you know, a bacon station is all the rage and I would seriously consider it if I were you."

"We'll take it under advisement," Sam said.

He took Maggie's elbow and led her into the house. Maggie tried not to tut at the muddy footprints on the floor, but Sam must have registered her unhappiness in the stiffening of her posture.

"We'll have a cleaning crew sweep through the house when we're done, I promise," he said.

Maggie listened for any creaks or door slams as they made their way through the house but with the noise coming from downstairs, it was impossible to discern.

"No lights have flashed, no doors have slammed and no ghosts have been sighted," Sam said as he started down the stairs to the basement.

"How'd you know what I was thinking?" she asked.

"Because I saw the concentration lines in between your eyes deepen," he said.

Maggie felt her forehead. "Wrinkles? Are you telling me I'm wrinkled?"

"Only when you worry," he said.

Maggie huffed out a breath. She knew he was right, which only made his observation all the more annoying.

Unlike her last time in the basement when just a flashlight had held back the gloom, this time great big floodlights filled the space, brightening up even the darkest corners. If there were any critters residing down here, Maggie was sure this ruckus would have driven them out into the back forty, so that was a plus.

Deputy Curtis was stationed by the storm doors at the far side of the basement. He waved when he saw Sam and Maggie and they waved back. A rolling cart had been set up outside the small root cellar and it was covered with equipment and supplies, among which Maggie noticed there was a body bag.

"You all right?" Sam asked.

"Fine," she lied.

Then she realized her fingers had tightened their grip on his and she forced herself to relax and loosen her hold.

"No, no, no, that's the wrong angle," a woman's voice barked from inside the root cellar. "We need a close-up of the fracture of the skull. Shine the light here and take the pictures from above."

Maggie glanced inside the room to see Andy, the woman she had seen with Sam earlier, shouting orders to two others. They all wore white coveralls and masks, as well as the same blue latex gloves Sam used when investigating a crime scene.

"They *are* planning on moving him, aren't they?" Maggie asked.

"Once they've fully recorded the scene," Sam said. "They'll take Captain Bones back to the lab for further analysis."

"Any clues yet as to what happened?"

"The crack on his skull is pretty telling, but Andy will have to be the one to decide for sure if it was a killing blow. She's the best, so I imagine she'll be able to tell us what killed him and hopefully who he was."

At the sound of her name, Andy whipped her head around and glanced at them.

"Sam!" she cried. "I was hoping you weren't going to miss the best part."

"Which would be what?" he asked.

"The extraction of the body," she said. She fairly glowed with excitement.

Maggie glanced down at Andy's feet but she didn't feel anything but relief that Captain Bones was going to be lodging elsewhere.

"Cool. Hey, come on out here for a sec," Sam said. "I want you to meet my fiancée."

Maggie saw the look on Andy's face when he said the word *fiancée*. It was fleeting but there was no doubt that her expression darkened with a whole lot of unhappy.

If what Sam said was true and Andy wasn't interested in him romantically then why did she care if he had a fiancée? The expression vanished so swiftly that Maggie wondered if she'd imagined it, but no, she knew dislike when she felt it. This woman did not like her at all.

"Andy, this is Maggie," Sam said. "Maggie, this is Andy, the best forensic pathologist in the state."

Andy looked pleased at the praise and she grinned at Sam. "Why, I bet you say that to all the forensic pathologists."

"Nope, just you," Sam said. He returned her grin.

"Well, coming from the best detective the Richmond PD ever had, I'll take that as very high praise," Andy said.

Maggie glanced between them, suddenly feeling like the third wheel on a bicycle built for two in the midst of their mutual admiration society.

"So, what can you tell us about our houseguest?" Maggie asked.

Andy glanced at her and then blatantly ignored her question. Instead, she pulled off her gloves and removed her cap and mask. The features Maggie had only glimpsed from afar before were now up close and horrifying. The woman had a head of thick, glossy black hair, a heart-shaped face that was defined by high cheekbones and arching eyebrows. She was, in a word, breathtaking.

Maggie glanced at Sam to see his reaction to the unveiling. He was still grinning at his friend and Maggie had a sudden urge to kick him.

"Hey, remember the time we got called out to the docks to retrieve a dead body out of the water?" Andy asked Sam.

He nodded with a chuckle. "Yeah, and the divers

couldn't get there in time so we had to fish him out with a borrowed rod and reel."

"He was the catch of the day," Andy joked and the two of them shared a knuckle bump and busted up laughing.

Maggie looked at them in horror.

"Sorry," Sam said, recovering first. "Gallows humor."

"Yeah, it keeps you from screaming in the middle of the night," Andy said. "But you have to be in the biz to understand."

Now they exchanged a grim look and, again, Maggie felt like quite the outsider. It was pretty clear that the two of them shared a long and grisly history.

"I'm going to grab some coffee," Sam said, and he gestured to the coffee pot in the corner. "Do either of you want some?"

"No, thanks," Maggie said.

"Yes, please," Andy said. She rubbed a hand over her eyes, and Maggie could see that she looked tired. "You know how I like it?"

"Of course," Sam said. "As thick and as black as tar and able to dissolve a spoon within ten minutes."

"Aw, you remembered," Andy said. "Thanks."

They watched him walk away and Maggie turned to Andy. She didn't know what to say to her, and she hated to admit it, but she felt intimidated by the other woman's occupation. Clearly, if Sam had called her the best, she was.

She decided to keep the conversation on Captain Bones—a neutral topic, she hoped.

"So, what can you tell me about our friend in there?" she asked.

Andy studied her for a moment. Her gaze was shrewd and Maggie had no idea what assumptions she was making about her. Maggie refused to knuckle under, however, and she maintained her eye contact with Andy. The woman must have sensed her determination, because Andy glanced at the root cellar and then back at Maggie. To Maggie's surprise, she answered her.

"It takes about fifty years for a body in a coffin deep in the ground to decompose and lose all of its tissue. I'd say this body was here are least seventy years and judging by the bits of uniform, which we'll have to verify, it looks to have been here since the Second World War. It's too early to say for sure, but the cranial fracture looks like it could have been a blunt head trauma and the cause of death."

Maggie nodded. She and Sam had figured as much but it was good to hear it confirmed. They were both quiet for a moment.

"You know Sam was the best detective on the Richmond PD, right?" Andy asked.

Maggie glanced across the basement where Sam was fixing two coffees and chatting with his deputy.

"Sam's good at whatever he does, so yeah, I figured as much," she said.

"Then you know what a waste it is to have him stuck in the middle of Podunk nowhere, spinning his wheels writing traffic tickets when he could be making a real difference," Andy said.

Now the flash of dislike Maggie had seen before on Andy's face was more than evident. She could feel the other woman's anger toward her but she had no idea how to talk her out of it.

"It was Sam's choice to retire—" she began but Andy interrupted.

"Sure, but he was bored after ten minutes here and seriously considering coming back until you came along," Andy said. "Make no mistake, I'm here to help my friend investigate a potential crime scene, but when I go back to Richmond I fully intend to bring Sam back with me."

Maggie was so shocked she was pretty sure she'd lost her powers of speech and that *never* happened. Here she'd thought that Andy wanted Sam back for a relationship and she'd been right. But it wasn't a romantic one, it was a working one.

"The man retired," she said. Her temper loosened her tongue enough to spit out the words. "Let him go already."

"Oh, but it's not me who's hanging on," Andy said. "It's him. Who do you think calls every week just to check in and see what cases we have cooking? He does. Why? Because he misses it. Look, I've got nothing against you or your cute little town, but that boy belongs in Richmond where he can be challenged by real cases and do what he loves. If you really love him, you'll encourage him to move back where he belongs whether you come with him or not."

Maggie felt as if Andy had just clocked her upside the head with a sledgehammer. Was it true? Was Sam unhappy in St. Stanley? She'd never lived anywhere else. Sure, she traveled but she always came home to St. Stanley. Always.

She felt Andy move away from her as she went back

into the root cellar with Captain Bones. She stared at Sam across the basement and watched him talking and laughing with one of the investigators from the county medical examiner's office. He really did look like he was in his element.

Was Andy right? Did Sam want to go back to Richmond? Could she walk away from everything she'd ever known and go with him? The thought made Maggie a bit queasy, mostly because they'd just bought this house and she'd just opened her own business.

Still, she didn't want to marry Sam and then, in a few months or weeks, have him up and leave her to go back to Richmond because he missed his job.

She glanced back at the root cellar and watched Andy ordering around her staff. Maggie straightened her spine. There was no way she was going to let this woman get inside her head. If Sam wanted to go back to Richmond, he would have told her by now. She was sure of it.

She took out her phone and sent a text to the Good Buy Girls. Yes, even Summer. Like it or not, she needed some of Summer's man advice. In fact, she needed all of their man advice.

Plus, she needed to get a handle on this wedding. If she didn't want to lose Sam then she had better make darn sure that they got hitched on the day they said they were getting hitched. And while it was okay for him to have just the two of them and Pastor Shields, she needed a little bit more in the witness box, especially if he was getting wobbly on her.

She glanced back at Andy. Sam had brought her coffee

to her and the two of them were laughing together again, no doubt some more gallows humor about the good old days. Well, that was fine. She didn't mind a little reminiscing, but there was no way she was going to let Andy infiltrate their wedding.

"You'll stop my wedding over my dead body," she muttered.

A cold draft blew across her skin and Maggie shivered. She glanced behind her to see if the storm doors were open and if that was where the breeze was coming from. No, they were shut. She glanced around the room and while the hair around her face still moved from the cool breeze, it appeared that the gust of air was circling her as everything else in the basement was completely undisturbed.

Maggie felt a gentle hand brush the hair out of her eyes. The only trouble was there was no one there. Maggie screamed.

Chapter 16

Everyone swiveled their heads in Maggie's direction. Sam started forward and she would have leapt into his arms except she saw Andy staring at her with clear contempt from the doorway of the root cellar.

Instead, she held up her hand to Sam to stop. She was not going to let Andy think she was a wimp, and she definitely wasn't going to admit to an otherworldly presence in the basement and have them all thinking she was a nutter.

"Sorry! I saw a snake," she said. Then she pointed toward the far corner. "It went that way."

In a move that locked Maggie's affection forever, Deputy Curtis jumped up onto a cinder block and scanned the surrounding area with his high-powered flashlight.

"Snake!" he cried in an unusually high-pitched voice. "I hate snakes!"

The others looked away from Curtis, some trying to hide their laughter and others making no attempt at all.

Curtis did not care. He spoke into his shoulder radio in a bark, "Deputies Wilson and Rourke, one of you will come down to the basement and relieve me immediately."

"Roger that," Deputy Rourke's voice answered.

Curtis looked at Sam. "I don't do snakes."

"Understood," Sam said. He put his arm around Maggie and she could feel his shoulders shaking as he was trying not to laugh.

She felt bad for needlessly scaring Curtis but not bad enough to admit what had really spooked her. Sam's warmth dispelled the chill that had crept under her skin and she was grateful.

"I think I'm going to be here awhile longer while they prep to move the body," Sam said. "Why don't you head home and I'll call you later."

"Sure," Maggie agreed. "I'll stop by your place and spend some quality time with Marshall Dillon."

"Why do I get the feeling you're avoiding going home and spending time with your mother?" he asked.

"Me?" Maggie put her hand on her chest in a protestation of innocence.

Sam smiled and kissed her. "I know your game, Maggie Gerber. Avoidance will not make the moms back off. In fact, it will only make things worse."

Maggie sighed. "I know. I promise I'll go home right after I tuck in Marshall Dillon."

Sam walked her out and Maggie felt a pang of regret that he was so preoccupied with excavating their house-guest. Yes, it had to be done. And, yes, they needed to know who the skeleton had once been, but she couldn't help feeling that they were charting a course of action that was going to change everything.

Maggie was true to her word. She did go back to her house after taking care of Marshall Dillon. Of course, it was not her fault that he seemed to require an inordinate amount of attention and he really felt the need to watch a movie with her while they shared a tub of popcorn.

And, oh darn, by the time Maggie got home, her mother was already asleep and she snuck in the back door just as she had all those years ago when she and Sam had been out and they'd broken curfew. What Mom didn't know then didn't hurt her and the same thing was true now. Or so Maggie told herself.

She did not count on waking up to find her mother sitting on the end of her bed, sipping coffee and doing the crossword while she waited for Maggie to wake up.

"Finally, look who decided to rise and shine," her mother said when Maggie blinked against the morning sun. Someone had opened her curtains. Oh, joy.

"I'm not rising or shining and you can't make me," Maggie said. Even to her own ears she sounded as if she were thirteen instead of in her early forties.

"Good thing I don't care if you're shining then," her

mother said. "But you will rise because we are going wedding dress shopping."

Maggie opened her mouth to protest, but her mother held up her hand.

"No arguments. This loosey-goosey thing you've got going for a wedding stops today."

Maggie didn't argue, protest, or even snivel. She knew her mother's "that's final" tone of voice when she heard it and she knew there would be no finagling, negotiating or wiggling out of this one.

"I really can't talk about this before co—" Maggie began to say but her mother pointed to her nightstand.

A fresh cup of coffee with a delicate puff of steam coming off the top in invitation sat waiting for her. She knew when she had lost.

She pushed herself up to a seated position and reached for the mug. It read World's Best Mom. Laura had given it to her when she was a kid and even though Maggie knew she was far from being the world's best anything, it touched her that her daughter had given it to her.

The coffee was just the way she liked it, with a little bit of milk and enough sugar to balance the bitterness of the brew. She glanced at her mother to give her thanks but stopped when she saw how intently her mother was studying her face.

"What? Do I have a pimple?" Maggie asked.

Her mother barked an unexpected laugh. "No. I was just thinking."

"Nothing good judging by your expression," Maggie

said. She was afraid her mother was about to confirm her words but figured it was best that they get it out in the open before they got any closer to the wedding.

"Actually, I was thinking just the opposite. You've dealt with so much and at such a young age. You worked so hard to take care of yourself and Laura and never wanted to lean on anyone. You and that little coupon pouch of yours, you've been through a lot."

"Old Blue," Maggie said with a smile. Yes, she had named her coupon holder. It was blue with mauve paisleys and she took it everywhere she went. She still did. In those early dark days, it had been a lifesaver.

Maggie wondered where this talk was going but she didn't want to interrupt her mother so she sipped her coffee and waited.

"Do you love Sam?" her mother asked. "Really love him for all that he is and all that he isn't?"

"Yes," Maggie said without hesitation.

"You're sure you're not in love with a boy from twenty-plus years ago who no longer exists?"

"I'm positive," Maggie said. "That boy grew up and so did the girl he loved."

"And your hesitation to plan your wedding is because why?"

There it was. The million-dollar question that only her mother had been brave enough to ask so directly. Maggie didn't have an answer.

"Is it because of Charlie?" her mother asked.

Maggie felt around in her insides. Was it Charlie that was holding her back? Did she have some loyalty to her late husband that kept her from being able to move forward with Sam?

"No," she said.

"Then what is it that's keeping you from picking flowers, a cake, a dress or a venue?"

Maggie blinked at her mother. "I don't know."

"You do want to get married, don't you?"

"Yes, of that, I am sure, but . . ." Maggie stalled.

"But what?" Lizzie asked. "Come on, spill it."

"I might be a little afraid of losing Sam like I lost Charlie," Maggie said. Her voice was barely above a whisper. "I just . . . I don't know if I could go through that again."

And just like that the dam burst and Maggie felt a sob burble up inside of her and tumble out of her mouth in one wrenching hiccup of stress.

"Oh, honey, I figured it was something like that." Lizzie took both of their coffee cups and put them aside, then she opened her arms and let Maggie cry it out just like she had when Maggie was seven and knocked her front teeth out on the monkey bars in the park.

She rubbed Maggie's back and made soothing noises and Maggie let herself be comforted. There was nothing like a mother's love to ease away the fear.

"Would you give him up just to keep yourself from the possible pain of losing him?" her mother asked.

"No," Maggie said. She pushed her hair back and met her mother's understanding gaze. "I won't give up what we have no matter what might happen."

Lizzie reached out and put her hand over Maggie's,

giving it a tight squeeze. "Then that settles it. It's time for you to jump all in, my girl. Now get up. We have dresses to try on."

Maggie groaned and sank deeper into her pillows. She couldn't make her get out of bed.

"I made cinnamon swirl coffee cake," her mother called over her shoulder as she left the room. Darn it. Her mom knew she couldn't resist her coffee cake.

"I look like I should be on *Dancing with the Stars*, the reject edition," Maggie said.

She was wearing a slinky blue gown that hugged her curves and dipped low in the front and in back and had a slit up the side to her upper thigh.

"Sam will love it," Joanne said.

"I love it," Summer said. "If you don't want it, can I have it?"

"Sure," Maggie said. It still jarred her to have Summer in her shop, joining her mother and sister and the Good Buy Girls while she tried on dress after dress. Fifteen had been rejected so far.

"It's all yours," Maggie said.

Summer clapped her hands and looked delighted. Yeah, it was definitely weird having her here.

"So what's the word on the skeleton in your house?" Ginger asked.

"Sam's colleague from the Richmond PD is trying to identify him," Maggie said. "As far as I know, there's been no word yet on who he is—er, was—or how he came to be in our basement."

"You're not still going to live there, are you?" Sissy asked. "I would have the willies, knowing there had been a dead body in my house."

"Don't be silly." Lizzie waved a dismissive hand. "Back in the day most people died at home in their own beds. Most of the houses in St. Stanley have had at least one dead body or more in them."

"Oh, ick," Summer said. "I'm telling Tyler we need to build a new home."

"You might want to stop by the library and check the old microfilm," Claire said. "The newspapers back in the day reported on a lot of the local goings-on, so you could probably find out quite a bit about the Dixons and their friends. If he was well known I bet someone wrote about him."

"That's an excellent idea," Maggie said. "Can I come by after I close the shop tonight?"

"Yes. I'm working the evening shift, so I can help," Claire said.

The bells on the door rang and Celeste Toovey entered the shop with her daughter.

Maggie made to go over and help them, but Joanne with baby Patience strapped to her front motioned for her to stay put.

"I got this," she said.

"Really? Because I would be so happy to take a break—"

"Just two more dresses," Lizzie interrupted. She pointed to the curtained-off area that acted as a dressing room. "Go."

Maggie tried to flounce away but the dress was too long and it just made her look like a little girl playing dress up, having a fit. She pulled the curtain closed behind her and glared at the last two dresses.

Why was this so difficult? She hadn't spent one-tenth of the time picking out her dress for her wedding to Charlie. Why was she having so much anxiety?

She stepped out of the slinky blue number with a sigh. Maybe she needed to see a therapist to get to the root of her dress dilemma. Could they do a quick fix on her in time for her to pick a dress and get married? She had a feeling that would be a no.

Maybe if she could just get one thing nailed down, like her dress or the flowers, then everything else would fall into place. It was clear that Sam figured if the two of them and the pastor were a go then they were all good. She supposed in the grand scheme of things he was right, but she knew she needed a little more pomp and circumstance to make it feel official. Plus, the mothers would never let her hear the end of it.

She pulled the sunflower-yellow dress over her head and prayed for a miracle. It came, but not in the yellow dress. Rather, it manifested in a surprise visit by Blue Dixon.

Chapter 17

Maggie heard the bells on the door jangle and she knew the Good Buy Girls would help whoever came in, but still it rankled that she was stuck here, trying on dresses when she should be manning her shop.

There were a few giggles and she wondered who it was that was charming the ladies. She even heard Summer's unique cackle so she figured it had to be a man. She moved the curtain aside to see if it was Sam. It was not.

Blue Dixon was holding court in her shop and he looked more than pleased to be in the midst of a flock of pretty-feathered ladies. Maggie wondered what had induced him to leave Spring Gardens and visit her. She knew they had talked about his checking out her suit collection but she really didn't think he'd come around.

Then again, maybe he'd had another altercation with Dennis Applebaum.

"Blue," she said as she stepped out of the curtained area. "It's nice to see you again."

"Afternoon, Maggie," he said. His blue eyes twinkled at her as he gestured at the ladies seated around him. "It appears I timed my arrival well."

She raised an eyebrow at him in what was supposed to be a quelling look but his grin only deepened.

"Your enchanting mother was just telling me that you are on a quest for a wedding dress," he said.

Maggie lifted the flouncy skirt of her yellow dress and gave them all a twirl. She could tell by the appalled expressions on all of their faces that this one was a unanimous reject.

"You look like a pat of butter," Summer said.

Maggie glared at her.

"What?" Summer asked. "Aren't girlfriends supposed to be honest?"

"Tact is always appreciated, too," Ginger said. "Besides she really looks more like a gob of mustard."

Summer blinked at Ginger and then hooted with laughter.

"Really, I thought she looked more like an ear of corn," Claire said.

This time they all laughed.

"Well, thank you all so very much," Maggie said in a huff. She lifted her skirts and made to disappear into the dressing room when Blue Dixon stopped her.

"My dear, do not let your friends' teasing bother you

for you are a vision in whatever you choose to wear. With that mane of glorious red hair and those striking blue-green eyes, you'll have your man tongue-tied and besotted with his first look at you."

"Aw," Joanne sighed. "That was lovely."

"It was," Maggie said. "Thank you, Blue."

He gave her a small nod.

"But that is not," Lizzie said. She waved at Maggie's dress as if she could make it vanish. "Go try on the last one."

The final dress, an A-line lavender number, did not win any votes for best dress either but at least it didn't warrant the endless food comparisons and fits of giggles.

By the time Maggie changed back into her clothes for the day, the crowd had dispersed as Joanne had to go put the baby down, Claire had to get back to work and Summer had to mind her own shop.

"Don't you fret," Ginger said as she gave Maggie a hug. "We'll find your dress."

"I don't see why you won't wear a white gown," Maggie's mother chided her. "This would all be so much easier if you'd just go traditional."

"Yeah, and you'd look like a corpse," Sissy said. "White's not your color. Stick to your guns, Sis."

Maggie hugged her mother and sister and shooed them out the door but not before her mother gave Blue one last flirtatious glance that he returned much to Maggie's horror.

"Do not romance my mother," she said to Blue. "You have enough ladies on your dance card."

"Yes, but I've always been partial to strawberry blondes," he said.

"It's a dye job," Maggie snapped.

Blue's smile deepened. "I like a woman who is invested in her appearance."

Maggie rolled her eyes. "I'm pretty sure you did not come by the shop to hit on my mother. So what can I do for you?"

"Actually, I'm looking to do a little business with you," he said. "You consign items, correct?"

"Yes," Maggie said. "Why?"

"After they passed away, Ida and Imogene's things were sorted and what didn't go to charity was put in a storage unit. There is a lot of furniture and dishes, some artwork and a few boxes of letters and photographs. I thought since you consign things, you might sell them for me."

"Are you sure?" Maggie asked. "Those are your family's belongings."

"I have everything that I want to keep, which are mostly memories now," he said. His tone sounded wistful. "When you get to be my age, you realize that things don't have as much value as moments in time. Memories can be savored forever but things, well, they just take up space and need to be dusted."

Maggie laughed. "I suspect you're right. I'd be happy to consign anything you'd like."

"Excellent," he said. "Tyler Fawkes is filling up the back of his truck as we speak and he'll be dropping the items off later today."

"You were pretty sure I'd take everything," Maggie said.

"You're a woman of business," he said. "Besides you like me."

Maggie smiled. "I do at that."

"Put in a good word for me with your mother then," he said. He put on the straw hat that rested on the counter beside him. "I'd be happy to escort her to your nuptials."

"I . . ." Maggie stuttered but Blue didn't wait to hear what she had to say. With a tip of his brim, he left her standing in the center of her shop, completely flummoxed.

"I'm just not sure he's exactly dateable," Maggie said into her phone while Tyler Fawkes unloaded box after box into her storeroom.

"Maggie, I am old enough to know my own mind," her mother said. "Besides I live in Florida. It's not like we could start up anything, you know, unless he moved."

"He's not going to move," Maggie said. "He has it too good in Spring Gardens."

"Hmm," her mother hummed and then executed a swift subject change. "Will you be home for dinner?"

"No, I'm going to stop by the library after I close up the shop."

"All right, we'll leave a plate for you. I think Sissy is roasting a chicken."

"Great, thanks," Maggie said. She made a mental note to pick up a sandwich from the deli on her way to the library. She'd had Sissy's chicken before. It was generally as parched as a desert in want of rain.

Tyler passed her as she switched off her phone. He was using a handcart to wheel in a vanity table and matching stool. He set them in the corner of the shop next to the tri-fold mirror that fastened to the top of the vanity.

"That is a beautiful piece," Maggie said.

"A classic white Louis XVI–style vanity," Tyler said.

Maggie gave him a surprised look and he gave his unshaven chin a rueful scratch as he explained, "Summer has one just like it."

"I thought for a minute there you were getting into antiques," Maggie said.

"No, I invest straight up in high tech," he said. "I do love the gadgets." He pointed back to the vanity. "You're going to need a locksmith to look at that. One of the drawers is locked but I didn't see a key to go with it, unless it's in one of those boxes."

Maggie nodded. She knew just who to call. "Thanks, Tyler. How much do I owe you?"

"No worries, Blue already paid me," he said. "Good thing, too, because Summer says I'm not allowed to charge friends for services rendered."

Maggie blinked at him. He scratched his beard again as an awkward silence fell between them.

"About Summer." He paused to clear his throat. "Thanks for letting her join you gals in your bargain hunting thing. It means the world to her."

Maggie shrugged. "We're still in the probationary period."

"I know," he said with a nod. "But she's changed. You'll see."

He looked so eager that Maggie didn't have the heart to tell him that she still found the whole thing weird. Did she see Tyler and Summer joining them for backyard barbecues? No, but then she'd never thought she'd live in the Dixon house, either, so life clearly had some surprises in store for her.

She picked up her phone and sent a text to the one person she knew would likely be able to get the stuck vanity drawer open. Then she found her box cutter and started unloading the haul from the Dixon house.

She had hoped that the boxes containing letters and photos would give her a clue as to the identity of the skeleton in the root cellar. There was nothing. Mostly, it was just clippings and photos of events that Ida and Imogene had been involved with over the years, such as the ladies' league, the local gardening club, etc . . .

The dishes were vintage as were many of the tchotchkes, like old glass ashtrays and a collection of porcelain dolls that Maggie knew would sell to the collectors who loved retro. She had recently begun selling items online, which was where most of her specialty items were sold.

She was just sorting a trunk full of old clothes when the door opened and her favorite boy genius walked in. Maxwell Button, in his early twenties with advanced degrees in art, physics and law, was one of Maggie's favorite people and in many ways the son she'd never had.

"So, what is this I hear that you and Sam are going

to get hitched at my old place of employment, the Frosty Freeze, with free dipped cones for everyone?" he asked.

"What?" Maggie squawked and smacked her head on the lid of the trunk as she rose out of it. "Ouch!"

"Oh, sorry," Max said. "I was just kidding."

"Very funny," Maggie said. She rubbed the back of her head and frowned at him. "Don't tell me you're trying to talk Bianca into tying the knot like that?"

"No, we'll have it at the house," he said. "She's pretty much had the whole thing planned out since she was five. All I have to do is show up in a tux."

"Oh." Maggie frowned, feeling a sudden spurt of envy at Bianca's decisiveness. "Still planning it for December?"

"She always wanted to be a winter bride," Max said. "It works for me. I want to take her to Paris as a wedding gift and this gives me time to save."

"Oh, she'll love that," Maggie said. She crossed the room and gave him a tight hug. "I'm so happy for you."

"Thanks," he said.

He grabbed at his short black hair as if he could pull it down over his face and hide. It seemed to Maggie it was just yesterday that he was the lanky, long-haired boy handing out cones at the Frosty Freeze while he studied quantum physics and Botticelli in his endless life quest for information.

"So, what did you need my help with?" he asked.

"I have a vanity table with a locked drawer and no key and since you're the best lock picker I know, I thought you could have a go at it," she said.

She gestured to the table and Max crossed the room to examine the vanity.

"Is it true that you found a skeleton in your new house?" he asked.

"Yes," Maggie said. "Don't tell me you didn't believe the gossip."

"Well, it seemed pretty far-fetched," he said.

"Like getting married at the Frosty Freeze? Gee, I wonder how these rumors get started."

"Touché," Max said with a laugh as he knelt before the stuck drawer. "Do you have a flashlight and a hairpin?"

"Of course," Maggie said and she went to retrieve the items.

She handed them to Max and then moved back to give him room to work. He stared into the keyhole with the flashlight. Then he inserted the hairpin. He turned it this way and that but it didn't budge.

"I think there might be some sort of glue in there," he said. "How about some nail polish remover and a cotton swab?"

"Let me check my supply kit," she said. Maggie hurried back into the break room and checked her tool box. Score! She had both. She took the items back out to Max.

"Just out of curiosity if I had asked for rat poison and a shovel . . . ?" he asked.

"You'd be out of luck on the poison, but I do have a shovel."

"That's not as reassuring as you might think," he said. "I use the nail polish remover to get the stickers and other ick off of dishes, picture frames, that sort of thing," Maggie said. "The shovel is a consignment item from Quentin Parsall, he seems to think it's valuable. And you never know when you're going to need a cotton swab."

"Clearly." Max dipped the swab in the nail polish remover and then put the whole swab into the lock and jiggled it. "This will take a minute to soak."

"Can I get you anything while you wait?" Maggie asked. "Pop, lemonade, coffee?"

"A cola would be great, thanks," Max said.

Maggie retrieved a cola for Max from the back room and grabbed a water for herself. She sat beside him on the floor while they waited. Max popped the top on his can and then gave her a sideways glance.

"What?" Maggie asked. "Do I have dirt on my face?"

"No," he said. "It's just that I heard another rumor that is truly too preposterous for words, but . . ."

"Fire away," Maggie said. "It can't be any crazier than some of the other things I've heard lately."

"Don't punch me in the mouth, okay?" he asked.

Maggie raised her eyebrows. "Because I'm known for punching people?"

"You might when you hear this one," he said.

"I promise no punching," she said.

"Cool. Okay, so I heard that Summer is now one of your Good Buy Girls, and I know that can't possibly be true."

"Well . . ." Maggie drew out the lone syllable until it was a five second whine.

"No. Just no," Max said. He looked appalled.

"It's on a purely trial basis," Maggie said.

"Because you hit your head and forgot that she tried to steal Sam and in fact ruined your first relationship with him?" he asked.

"Hey, when did you get so judgy?" Maggie asked. "You're the one who defended her when she was in jail for murder."

"Only because her mother paid me really, really well," Max said. "I've never forgotten how she befriended Bianca's crazy step sister when she tried to take away Bianca's inheritance."

"So she had poor taste in friends," Maggie said. "She's trading up now."

"I do not believe this," Max said.

"I know, it's weird," Maggie agreed. "But Tyler said she's changed."

"He's her husband, of course he said that," Max argued. "Besides he's been in love with her for years. He's never had clear vision when it comes to his wife."

"Agreed," Maggie said. "But I promised I'd give her a chance."

"You must be crazy in love with Sam," he said.

"What makes you say that?" Maggie asked. "You know, other than us getting married."

"Because only a person in love could forgive all of the crap that Summer has dumped on you all these years."

"I like to think I gave as good as I got," Maggie said.

Max laughed. "Yeah, you did at that. Just be careful, Maggie. You're one of my favorite people, and I don't want to see you get hurt."

"I will be, I promise," she said.

Max seemed satisfied and he put aside his soda and returned his attention to the drawer. He removed the swab and then resumed his work with the flashlight and the hairpin.

Maggie felt herself tense. What could be in the drawer that had required the lock being glued shut? The dreamer in her couldn't help but wonder if it was something precious like a rare strand of pearls, or an emerald ring as big as a walnut. Or maybe it was some old stocks and bonds that would be worth a fortune now. Of course, she'd have to give it all to Blue, but still the idea of discovering a treasure made her all fluttery inside.

Max jiggled the hairpin back and forth and then he nudged it in deeper. Suddenly, there was a click and the drawer popped just a smidge.

"Got it!" Max cried in triumph.

Together they rose up on their knees as Max slid the drawer open. No diamond necklace or wad of cash glittered out at them and Maggie sighed.

"Seems like a lot of work to keep people from finding a dried up flower and a glove," Max said ruefully.

"Agreed," Maggie sighed.

She reached into the small drawer and removed what looked like it had once been a wrist corsage but was now a shriveled up bunch of weeds tied with a lilac ribbon. Below that rested a delicate kid glove. It was yellowed with age but still buttery soft to the touch. The small pearl buttons shone against the dullness of the leather.

"I think this must have been where Ida Dixon kept her treasures," she said. "The sentimental ones."

"How do you know it's Ida's vanity and not Imogene's?" Max asked.

"From what I've read, Imogene was not the vanity type," she said.

She reached farther into the drawer and pulled out a packet of cards. As she sifted through the yellowed papers, she noted they were addressed to Ida and were from birthdays and graduations, as well as other events in the young woman's life.

"Do you need me for anything else?" Max asked, bringing Maggie back to the present.

"No, but thank you so much," she said. As she stood a small card fluttered from the pile in her hands.

"Here," Max said. He stooped down to get it and handed not a card but an old sepia photograph to Maggie.

She glanced at it and caught her breath.

"Maggie, are you all right?" Max asked as he gripped her elbow as if afraid she was going to keel over.

"Huh?" Maggie stared at the photo and then at Max. "What?"

"Are you all right?" he asked again. He looked worried. "You went so pale. Do I need to call Sam?"

"I'm fine, better than fine," Maggie said. She looked at him and held up the picture. "I think we just found our skeleton in the basement."

Chapter 18

Maggie called Sam but she got his voice mail. It picked up on one ring so he was clearly talking to someone else. She didn't want to explain over the phone so she left a message asking him to call her.

She kept studying the photograph of the young couple—a woman in a flared-skirt day dress and a man in uniform—as if they would tell her who they were. It was killing her to not be able to ask anyone about the photo. There were no clues on it other than the notation of the year 1944 which had been written in blue ink on the back in the lower right-hand corner.

Max watched her study the photograph while she paced. Finally, he sighed and said, "Maggie, you're going to wear a hole in the floor. Do you want me to watch the shop while you go give the photo to Sam?"

"Would you?" Maggie cried. "That would be so great!"

"No problem," he said. "I figure I still owe you a favor or two from the old days."

Maggie kissed his cheek, grabbed her purse and hustled to the door. "I'll be back in an hour at the latest."

She hurried to her Volvo station wagon that was parked at the corner. Since she had one stop to make before she went to see Sam she figured it would be faster if she drove.

It was less than five minutes to get across town and pull in at Spring Gardens. She signed in at the main desk and then hurried through the lobby to the pool. She had been hoping to find Blue with his bevy of gray-haired beauties in his usual spot but no luck. She turned and hurried back to the main desk.

"I'm sorry, can you tell me where I might find Blue Dixon?" she asked.

"He's not poolside?" the pretty brunette with a name tag that read ANNE asked.

Maggie shook her head.

"Oh, I see why." The girl looked at her clipboard.

Maggie had a sudden heart-pounding fear that Blue might have up and died. Is that what the clipboard was, a clipboard of death?

"He's in the pool tournament in the rec room," Anne said. "I heard he and Dennis Applebaum are trying to work out their differences through a friendly pool match."

"Which way?" Maggie asked.

"Down the hall and to your right." Anne pointed.

Maggie jogged toward the room. Dennis and Blue had already been to Doc Franklin for one round of injuries. Who was the knucklehead who thought it was a good idea to give them long wooden sticks to play with? Maggie had visions of finding one or the other of them impaled on his pool cue.

She pushed through the double doors into the rec room to find a crowd had gathered around the pool table. A quick glance and Maggie could see that there were two solid balls, two striped balls and the eight ball. Dennis was lumbering around the table with a swagger that made Maggie think he had just sunk one.

"Lucky shot," Blue muttered, confirming her guess.

"Seven in the corner," Dennis said and pointed with his cue.

He missed and Blue looked thrilled. He clapped his hands together as if relishing the prospect of demolishing his opponent. As he moved around the table, Maggie elbowed her way past the front row of spectators.

"Blue, I need to talk to you," she said.

"Maggie, I'm in the middle of something," Blue protested.

"Sorry, but I have no time and this is really important," she said.

Blue glanced at Dennis. "Five minutes?"

"If that's what you need to build up your courage," Dennis said with a careless shrug.

"Hey!" Blue started to protest but Maggie dragged him away.

"Bigger issues, Blue," she said.

"To you maybe," he grumbled. "My reputation is at stake here."

Maggie fished the picture out of her purse. "Do you know this man?"

Blue looked from her to the picture. "No, but I know the woman. That's my cousin Ida Dixon."

"Are you sure?" Maggie asked.

"Positive. Where did you find that?"

"It was in the vanity table in a drawer that was glued shut."

Blue leaned on his pool cue and rubbed his chin with the back of his hand. "Glued? I thought it was just locked and the key was missing."

"It was locked and glued," Maggie said.

"Strange," Blue said. His eyes had a far-off look in them and Maggie wondered what he was thinking.

A crash sounded from the other side of the room and they both started and glanced over at the pool table.

"No! Stop! Argh!" Dennis cried. "This is no place for children! Who let this demon spawn in here?"

"Uh-oh," Blue said and he hurried back to the table.

A towheaded boy about five years old was holding two of the pool balls in his chubby fists. He glanced up at everyone and a big fat tear pooled in his right eye.

"Is this saboteur yours, Dixon?" Dennis asked.

"No, and quit yelling," Blue snapped. "You're scaring

the poor kid." Blue looked at the boy and said, "It's all right. It's just a game, but next time, ask before you take things that don't belong to you."

A sweet older lady gave Blue an adoring look before she enfolded the little boy in an embrace and wiped away his tears.

"Seems to me you should follow your own advice," Dennis said as he placed his cue in the rack.

Blue rolled his eyes at him. "I demand a rematch."

Dennis crossed over to where they stood. "Fine by me."

He glanced at Maggie. "You didn't have anything to do with this, did you?"

"No," Maggie said. She raised her hands in a gesture of innocence.

Dennis frowned at the photo. "Why do you have a picture of Jasper Kasey?"

Maggie glanced from Dennis to the photo. "Excuse me?"

"Jasper Kasey," Dennis said. He tapped the picture with his forefinger. "I'd know him anywhere. My brother and I followed Captain Kasey around like puppies. He was a pilot in World War Two. We thought the sun rose and set on him. Who's the dame?"

"My cousin Ida," Blue said stiffly.

"Ah, well, there's no accounting for taste," Dennis said.

Blue balled up a fist and looked like he was going to pop Dennis, but Maggie looped her arm through his and held him back.

"Thank you, Dennis, you've been a huge help," she said.

"Any time," Dennis said. "You can always count on me when he lets you down."

Blue shifted and Maggie snatched the cue out of his hand right before it would have bopped Dennis on the back of the head.

"Stop that!" she hissed. "You're behaving like a child."

"Can't help it," Blue grumbled. "That guy just brings out the toddler in me, and in my defense I have had to spend more time with him and his brother than a sane person should. I know Doc Franklin wanted me to help them with the ladies but I'm pretty sure I'd have better luck with a pair of goats. "

He puffed out his lower lip and it was all Maggie could do not to laugh. "He also gave me my best clue of the day, so be nice. The uniform Jasper's wearing is the same one the skeleton had on."

"What?" Blue studied the photo more closely. "You think this guy is the skeleton in your basement."

"It seems likely," Maggie said.

Blue studied the picture. "It looks like she loves him, doesn't it?"

"Yes, it does," she agreed.

In the photo, Ida was smiling up at the handsome captain and it was easy to see that she was completely enamored with him. The smile on his face was less giddy but no less warm. Maggie had a feeling that he loved Ida in return.

"But if his skeleton is in the basement, then that means . . ." Blue paused and then he looked severe. "Ida didn't kill him."

He said it with a stubborn conviction that Maggie knew would never be swayed. Blue was obviously fond of his late cousin and he was going on the offensive to protect her good name.

"No one said she did," she reminded him. "Knowing his identity is just the start to finding out who may have wanted to harm him. I'm going to turn this over to Sam and he'll take it from there."

"Tell him, well, I'd like that picture back when he's done," Blue said. He looked rueful. "I forgot how carefree and happy she was when she was younger."

Maggie nodded and squeezed his arm. "I'll make sure you get it back. In the meantime, behave yourself."

Blue glared at the door through which Dennis had departed. "It won't be me who picks the fight."

"Just make sure it's you who stays out of the fight," she said.

"Fine," Blue said. He sounded very put out about it but Maggie didn't have time to argue with him any longer.

A glance at her phone and she knew she was cutting it close to get back to the shop within the hour. She definitely did not want to impose on Max, who, as a practicing attorney, had enough demands upon his time.

Fifteen minutes was all she could spare. She hurried to her car and drove over to the police station. She parked in the lot and ran up the walk.

"Who lit your tail feathers on fire?" Deputy Dot Wilson asked as Maggie slammed through the front door.

"No time," Maggie huffed. "I have to see Sam."

"Is everything all right?" Dot asked. She came around

the desk to open the half door that would let Maggie in the back.

Dot was built stout, which she often said was to shoulder the problems she dealt with every day. But she managed to make herself feminine with attention to the details like makeup and jewelry. It was always done with a light hand, but still, she came across as polished and pretty instead of as someone who had given up. She was one of Maggie's favorite people and not just because her shoe obsession brought her into Maggie's shop on a regular basis.

"It's better than okay," Maggie said. She waved the photo. "I have something to show Sam."

Dot's eyebrows lifted. "About your tenant in the root cellar?"

"The same," Maggie said.

"I want to hear this," Dot said and she followed Maggie to Sam's office.

Maggie could hear voices as they approached spilling out from the door that was open just a crack.

"Remember when Lufkowitz lost his watch to that hooker outside the coffee shop on Parker Ave?" Andy asked. She was hooting with laughter and Maggie could hear Sam chuckling as well.

"Yeah, and his biggest concern was how to tell his wife, since she had just given it to him for their anniversary," Sam added. He laughed harder and Andy banged on the edge of his desk with her fist as she doubled up, giggling uncontrollably.

"And he actually . . . hid . . . under his desk," Andy gasped.

The two of them were having fits now and Maggie and Dot stood in the doorway watching them.

"It's been like this ever since she got here," Dot said. "You'd think they were party planners for the dang circus the way they carry on about how great the old days were."

Dot sniffed and Maggie could tell her nose was a bit out of joint over the boss reminiscing so much about his former place of employment.

"I'm sure it will pass," Maggie said. "Eventually."

"Uh-huh." Dot sounded doubtful. Then she glared at Sam and raised her voice over their ruckus. "Sheriff, if you have a minute, your fiancée actually has the first clue that might help you out with your investigation."

"Huh . . . what?" Sam wiped the tears of mirth from his face and glanced at the door. "Oh, hey, Maggie, when did you get here?"

"A few minutes ago," Maggie said. Her lips moved into a smile position but it felt thin, like when she was low on butter and tried to spread what little she had across an entire piece of toast. It never tasted right.

"So, what's this about a clue?" he asked.

Andy was still laughing, paying no attention to them, and Maggie got the feeling she was going to roll right into another "remember when" moment.

Maggie held up the photo to stop the other woman from speaking. "Look at this. See anything familiar about this guy?"

Sam took the photo and Dot moved to look over his shoulder, refusing to budge when Andy crowded in behind her.

"That's the uniform—" he began but Maggie interrupted.

"—that's on Captain Bones," she said. "Except thanks to this photo I now know his real name is Jasper Kasey."

Chapter 19

Sam's eyes went wide and he hugged her close. "Look at you! I may have to put you on the payroll as a detective, darling."

He gave her a smacking kiss on the lips and Maggie saw Dot grin while Andy looked like she'd bit a lemon.

"Not to be a doubter, but how do you know that's the same man? And how did you get his name?" Andy asked. Her voice was dubious with a dash of condescension, and Maggie found she didn't much care for the other woman's attitude.

"Since selling the house to us, Blue Dixon has decided to empty out the old storage unit where he kept the sisters' belongings," Maggie said. "One of the items was an old vanity table that belonged to Ida Dixon, the woman in the photo."

"Wow, I only knew her as an old woman," Sam said as he studied the photo. "She was quite a looker in her day."

"She looks like she loved him," Maggie said.

"That's hardly a scientific assessment," Andy said. She tossed her long dark hair over her shoulder.

Maggie frowned at her. "As for the identity of the man, Dennis Applebaum gave me his name when I stopped by Spring Gardens to show the photo to Blue, who identified his cousin Ida. By the way, Blue asked if he could have it back when you're done with it."

"Of course," Sam said.

"So, how many people have handled the photograph?" Andy asked.

"A few," Maggie said. "Me, Blue, Dennis and now Sam."

"Well, that's going to muddy up any fingerprints that we might have found."

"I doubt that Ida Dixon had ever been fingerprinted in her lifetime," Dot Wilson said. "So, I don't see how it would have helped anyway."

Maggie sent her a grateful look. She didn't think she was imagining that Andy was being a bit of a jackass about the whole thing. It was almost as if she resented Maggie for finding a bit of vital information.

Sam fished through his desk drawer. He pulled out a large magnifying glass and held it over the photo.

"Dennis was right," he said. "You can just make out the name on his uniform. Kasey."

Maggie looked through the magnifier. She felt a thrill course through her at having found out the identity of their skeleton.

"I guess we'll have to call him Captain Kasey or Jasper now," she said. "I have to stop by the house on my way to the library to pick up our sleeping bags for Sandy. I'll be sure to salute."

"Do." Sam smiled at her. For a moment it felt as if no one else was even in the room with them. "Nice work, darling," Sam said and he winked at her.

"Thank you," she said.

"And now the professionals will make sure it's actually accurate," Andy said.

"I'm sure it is, but let's see if the military has records on Captain Jasper Kasey that they can share with us to confirm his identity," Sam said. "You have been in touch with them already, right? Since we found a soldier in uniform, it was your first move, correct?"

"Well, I . . . not having an office has made it difficult," Andy hedged.

Sam gave her a hard look and Maggie saw Andy squirm just a little bit.

"You are being paid for this investigation," Sam said. "I would expect you to treat it with the same professionalism as any other."

Andy shot Maggie an irritated look and then nodded. "Of course."

"Deputy Wilson, help Ms. Lowenstein settle into the empty office down the hall," he said. He turned to Andy and said, "Dot can get you anything you need."

"Thanks," Andy said. She left the room behind Dot, looking duly chastised.

Sam watched them go with a considering look on his face. Maggie wondered if this was the time to mention that Andy's motivation was to encourage him to go back to Richmond, but then she hesitated. Did she want to influence his decision or let him make up his own mind?

"Dennis Applebaum, huh?" Sam asked.

Maggie decided to let the moment pass. "Yeah, can you believe it?"

"I've missed you," Sam said as he pulled her close.

"Same here," Maggie said. "Are you on duty tonight?"

"Until eleven," he said. "Meet me at my place then?"

Sam gave her a wicked smile that made her think of tussled bed sheets and hot sheriffs—well, her hot sheriff.

"Sounds like a plan," she said. She glanced at the clock on the wall. "Uh-oh, gotta go. I left Max watching the shop."

She kissed Sam swiftly on the lips and bolted for the door.

Maggie closed and locked her shop at eight o'clock. Her niece Sandy had texted her earlier in the day, saying that they needed the sleeping bags Maggie and Sam had used on their campout in the house for more relatives who were coming for the wedding.

It was still light out, barely, so Maggie figured she'd swing by the house and grab the sleeping bags on her way to the library. She hadn't thought she'd get a ton of research done before the place closed and hoped that Claire had already managed to narrow down the amount of microfiche she'd be looking through tonight.

She parked in the driveway and noted that a light was on in the house. It was the one she and Sam left on for security. At least she hoped it was that one and not the ghost being funny and running up their electric bill. She crossed the porch and unlocked the door.

"Hello!" she called.

There was no answer. Not that she had been expecting one. Captain Kasey had been transported to the medical examiner's office for further investigation so there was really no reason for anyone to be here in the house. Still, it seemed only polite to call out a greeting.

She shut the door behind her and walked across the wood floor. She caught herself tiptoeing and then stopped, making herself walk normally.

She cleared her throat and said, "Good evening, Captain Kasey. I'm not sure if you're still here if your skeleton isn't, but I just want you to know that Sam and I are going to figure out what happened to you."

She paused, waiting to see if the light flickered or if the doors banged open and shut. Maybe he had left with his skeleton, after all.

"Well, I just wanted you to know that," Maggie said. Her eyes darted around the empty front room, but again, there was nothing. Maybe everything she had seen before had just been the weather and the old house settling, like Sam said.

She picked up the sleeping bags where they'd left

them rolled up in front of the fireplace. She could see herself here, reading a book by the fire in the winter with Marshall Dillon curled up in her lap. Maybe buying this old place hadn't been that crazy after all.

She checked the doors and windows on the lower floor to make sure it was secure before carrying the sleeping bags out the front door. She paused to lock the door before adjusting the bags in her arms and striding across the porch.

She had just reached the top step when her leg caught and she was sent sprawling forward down the steps and onto the hard concrete walkway. Thankfully the sleeping bags cushioned her fall, keeping her from breaking her neck or anything else she'd rather not have broken.

She lay face down on the sleeping bags, trying to regain her composure. She hated to think it but had she been pushed? There was no one here besides her, so that left the presence in the house. Was it trying to hurt her?

Maggie glanced back at the house half expecting to see a ghoul peering at her from one of the windows. Then she shivered.

Chapter 20

The light from the street illuminated something on the top step. Maggie pushed herself to her feet and moved closer to check it out. Fishing line had been strung six inches above the top step. That was what had made her fall, not the bad intentions of an irritable ghost.

She supposed this should have made her feel relieved but instead her head whipped from side to side to see if anyone was lurking in the shadows.

She pulled her phone out of her pocket and dialed Sam's direct number.

"Hey there, darling." Sam's deep voice instantly soothed Maggie, wrapping its warm affection around her like a down jacket on a cold night.

"Hi, Sam," she said.

"What's wrong?" he asked. Something in her tone must have demonstrated her upset because he was immediately on alert.

"I'm at the house and need you to come by," she said.

"Are you safe?" he countered.

"Yes," she said. She glanced around the front yard. "At least, I think so."

"Don't hang up," he said. "I'm a few blocks over but I can be there in five minutes."

Through the receiver she heard him use his radio to call into the station. She supposed it was ridiculous because if anything happened to her there really wasn't anything Sam could do but she felt better just having a connection to him.

"What happened? Is everything okay in the house?" he asked.

Maggie knew that was his way of asking if she'd seen a ghost without him asking if she'd seen a ghost, which he couldn't bear to do since he was such a skeptic. She smiled.

"The house is fine," she said. "No creaks, flickers or moans."

"Good," he said. "Or maybe I would prefer that?"

"I think you might," she said. "It looks like someone stopped by while I was inside and left me a surprise."

"Hang on," he said. "I'm pulling up now."

"I'm on the walk in front of the house," Maggie said. "I see you."

Maggie ended the call as Sam climbed out of his squad car and strode across the lawn toward her. He looked at the sleeping bags on the ground and then at her.

"Camping out tonight?" he asked as he gave her a swift hug.

Maggie gave him a lopsided smile. "Actually, they saved me from breaking my neck or my face, depending on how I would have fallen."

Sam frowned.

"While I was inside, getting the sleeping bags for Sandy, someone rigged up fishing line across the top step," Maggie said. "I did a lovely face-plant on the side-walk but since I was holding the sleeping bags in my arms, they cushioned my fall."

Sam moved forward and examined the line. "What the hell?"

"That's what I said. It wasn't there when I got here so it had to be someone who saw me go into the house, and they strung it while I was inside, chatting with the spirit of Captain Kasey."

Sam turned to look at her.

"It seemed only polite," she said.

"I love you," he said.

"I know," she said. "I love you, too."

"I'm going to scout the yard," he said. "Stay here and yell if you need me."

Maggie nodded. While Sam disappeared around the side of the house, she picked up the sleeping bags and carefully stepped over the fishing line and sat on the porch.

She couldn't hear Sam as he walked the perimeter.

The only sounds she could hear were that of the birds still chattering before they settled in for the night and the gossiping chirp of crickets. There were no strange noises coming from the house or the street.

Sam was back shortly. He had a flashlight in hand that he switched off as he approached.

"I don't like this," he said. He stepped over the fishing line and sat beside Maggie. "It's too specific to be random."

"What do you mean?"

"Whoever did this knew you were in the house," he said. "They did this with the intent to harm you. Not severely but it could have gone very badly."

"Bored teenagers?" Maggie suggested.

"Unlikely," he said. "No, this has to have something to do with Captain Kasey."

"But he's been moved," Maggie said. "Why harm us now?"

"An injury would slow down the investigation," he said.

"And our wedding," Maggie said. She wondered if now would be a good time to mention that Andy had expressed her determination to bring Sam back to Richmond with her.

"Nothing is going to slow down our wedding," Sam said. "If I have to walk a mile on broken glass, I'm going to marry you."

"Aw, that's so sweet," Maggie teased.

Sam laughed and wrapped his arm around her shoulders and pulled her close. "That's because I mean it."

And just like that Maggie had a lump in her throat and

felt her love for this man expand even though she was sure she couldn't love him any more than she already did.

"I'd do the same for you," she said. "I love you."

"I know," he answered.

They were quiet for a moment.

"What do we do now?" Maggie asked.

"You go home. I know you planned to go to the library, but I'd prefer you wait on that until we have a better handle on this," he said. "I'm going to get my fingerprint kit and see if I can pull any prints off of the railing. Then I'm going to canvass the neighborhood and see if anyone saw anything during the time you were in the house. Lastly, I am going to see if anyone has any security cameras that might cover this part of the street, but that's a long shot."

"You're really good at this," Maggie said. She'd always known he was but somehow watching him "protect and serve" their home made her appreciate his skills all the more.

"Thank you, I try," he said.

He gave her a humble look and Maggie felt a pang in her chest. Suddenly she had to know.

"Do you miss it?" she asked.

"Miss what?"

"Being a detective in the big city where there were so many cases and so many more opportunities for investigation?"

Sam was quiet for a moment, considering her words. When he spoke his voice was low and full of feelings that Maggie hadn't heard in him before. She had to untangle the emotional rope they were twined into and when she did she felt the threads of despair, frustration, disgust and horror twist in her palm like a live snake.

"No," he said. "I don't miss it. For every successful investigation, there were at least five failures. The scale was out of balance and no matter how hard I worked I could never seem to tip it in favor of the good guys. There may be less drama here but there is also less pain, a lot less pain."

Maggie squeezed his hand in hers, letting him know she understood. Sam pulled her to her feet and scooped up the sleeping bags.

"Come on," he said. "I'll walk you to your car."

With a kiss, a hug and a wave Sam sent her on her way. Maggie hadn't expressed her one remaining concern with Sam, but now after his confession that he did not miss the big city detective life, she wondered if she should have.

But how was she supposed to mention, casually in conversation, that the only people who knew she was going to the house tonight had been him, her niece, Sandy, Deputy Wilson and Andy Lowenstein?

The next morning Maggie arrived at the historical society bright and early. She hadn't been able to sleep the night before because she couldn't stop thinking about the fishing line tied across the top step. Frankly, it creeped her out to think that someone had done that while she was in the house. To what purpose?

Sam had struck out on any witnesses or security cameras picking up anything unusual in the neighborhood. As much as Maggie would have been okay with blaming Andy for the stunt, in her heart of hearts, she just didn't believe the other woman was capable of hurting her to get what she wanted. That left her thinking that whoever had strung the line across the porch had done it as a warning or a disruption.

When she thought of what she might have broken because of the mean stunt, she was resolved to figure out who was responsible. In the old days, her first thought would have been Summer. Okay, her only thought would have been Summer. But she didn't think so now. It just didn't fit. Why would Summer care about the house or the skeleton or any of it?

No, the only reasonable explanation was that it had to do with the house and Jasper Kasey's skeleton.

The door to the historical society was open. Mary Lou Sutton was manning the desk in the corner of the room. Maggie was relieved to find her there instead of Ruth. She wasn't up for another lecture on maintaining the historical integrity of her house.

"Hi, Mary Lou," she said. She held out the books she was carrying. "I'm just returning some books that Ruth lent me."

"Oh, well, thank you," Mary Lou said. She took the books and put them on the edge of her desk. She looked at a note on her desk, back at the books and then at Maggie. "I'll make sure these get back on the shelf, but, um, my note here says you had three books."

"That's right," Maggie said.

"You only handed me two," Mary Lou said. She made a face like she hated to break the bad news to Maggie that she was the worst borrower ever.

"Oh no. I forgot one," Maggie said. "Can I bring it by later?"

"That'd be fine," Mary Lou said. "Did you find out what you needed?"

"I did," Maggie said. "But I have more questions."

Mary Lou laughed. "Isn't that always the way with historical research? You find one answer and then have three more questions."

"It sure is," Maggie agreed. "I'm particularly interested in a man named Jasper Kasey."

"Isn't that the skeleton that was found in your house?" Mary Lou asked. She looked sheepish. "Sorry, it's a small town and word travels fast."

"No, it's all right," Maggie said. "The investigator is trying to verify who it is. She hasn't determined that it is Jasper Kasey yet."

"But you wanted to read up on him just in case," Mary Lou said. "I get that."

She rose from behind her desk and walked Maggie over to a vertical file along the wall.

"This is a biographical index of all of the people who have resided in and around St. Stanley for as long as we can remember," Mary Lou said. "It's part of my job to keep it up to date."

Maggie had no idea such a thing existed. Mary Lou opened a drawer and Maggie could see that it was file after file of clubs, organizations and prominent citizens over the years. She pulled out the Girl Scout troop folder for the years her daughter had been a member and sure enough the file contained the troop roster and Laura Gerber was listed.

"This is incredible," Maggie said.

"It is pretty special," Mary Lou said. "I collect all of the club rosters, club memberships, and clip out any biographical articles from the weekly paper. As a backup, I've been scanning the really old documents into an online database, but I've only gotten through the Cs."

"That is a huge undertaking," Maggie said.

"It's what they pay me for," Mary Lou said.

"Not enough."

Mary Lou laughed. "No, I enjoy it. It's fascinating to read about the people who have lived in our small town."

"Does the library know you're doing this?" Maggie asked.

"Oh yes," Mary Lou said. "Claire and I plan to make the database available at the library once it's finished."

Maggie nodded. She might have known that Claire would already have a stake in the research tool.

Mary Lou thumbed through the file folders before her. She turned back to Maggie with an apologetic face. "Sorry, but we don't appear to have a file folder for Jasper Kasey."

Maggie pushed down her disappointment. "Well, it was worth a shot. Do you suppose he'd be listed in any of the folders for clubs and organizations? Particularly anything from the late thirties and early forties."

Mary Lou tapped her index finger to her lips while she thought about it. "He was military, right?"

"Yes," Maggie said. "Air Force or at least I was told by Dennis Applebaum that he was a pilot."

Mary Lou opened a different drawer and flipped through several folders. She pulled out a wide folder and laid it open on the top of the cabinet. Maggie could see there were lists of names and some had stars beside them.

"The ones with stars mean they were killed in battle," Mary Lou explained. "This is a list of all of the veterans in the county from the Civil War to date."

Maggie leaned in to get a look at the file.

"Here's World War Two," Mary Lou said. She was running her finger down the list. "Well, that's odd."

"What?" Maggie asked.

"A name has been whited out," Mary Lou said. "And it's exactly where Jasper Kasey would fall in the roster."

Chapter 21

"May I see?" Maggie asked.

Mary Lou handed her the paper and sure enough in between Edward Higgins and Martin Lewis a name had been very carefully covered with Wite-Out.

"That's weird, right?" Maggie asked.

Mary Lou shrugged. "It could have been an error, but yeah, it seems odd."

"I'm going to need to bring this to Sheriff Collins so he can take a look at it," Maggie said. "Maybe he can find out what's beneath the Wite-Out."

Mary Lou bit her lip. "I'd have to ask Ruth first. She doesn't like anything in the file to leave the building."

"This is a police investigation," Maggie said. "I don't see that she has much choice."

"Choice about what?"

Maggie and Mary Lou spun around to see Ruth approaching, and she did not look happy.

"There's an item here that needs to be shown to the sheriff," Maggie said.

She was pleased that her voice was smooth and not as rattled as she felt given that Ruth was looking at her with blatant suspicion.

"Why does Sheriff Collins need to see it?" Ruth snapped. "What are you looking for specifically?"

"I was looking for information about a World War Two fighter pilot named Jasper Kasey," Maggie said. She studied Ruth's face for any hint of recognition. There was none. "We found where his name should be on the list of veterans from St. Stanley, but it's been Wited-Out. Who would do that?"

Ruth glanced at the list. This time Maggie saw her lips get tight. "No one covered up the name if that's what you're insinuating. More than likely, it was a typo. Things weren't done on computers back then."

Maggie gave her a hard stare. "Maybe not, but if it isn't Jasper Kasey's name under the Wite-Out, whose was it?"

"No one's," Ruth said. "This list was typed up long after World War Two, clearly whoever did it twenty or thirty years ago made a simple mistake."

"There's nothing simple about this," Maggie said. "Not if they were covering up a murder."

Ruth gasped as if Maggie had slapped her. "Are you calling into question the integrity of the historical society?"

"No, just its members'," Maggie said.

Two red spots of color brightened Ruth's rouged cheeks, making her look as if she were being lit up on the inside by her anger.

"That was uncalled for," Ruth said. Her voice was barely above a whisper.

She blinked at Maggie from behind her round spectacles and Maggie had the uncomfortable feeling that Ruth was going to cry. Guilt swamped her. When had she become a bully?

"I'm sorry," Maggie said. "You're right. I was out of line. This whole situation with the house has made me very tense."

Ruth bobbed her head vigorously as if she couldn't agree more that Maggie was behaving very badly.

"I'm going to take this list to Sheriff Collins," Maggie said. "I think he'll be able to have someone look at it and tell us what is under the Liquid Paper."

Ruth opened and closed her mouth, but no sound came out. When Maggie went to take the paper from Mary Lou, she clutched it close.

"Can I make a copy of it before you go?" Mary Lou asked. "I haven't had a chance to enter it into the database and if anything happened to it . . ."

"Nothing will happen," Maggie said. "I promise."

"It's critical that we not lose this list of names," Mary Lou insisted. "Beyond your own interests, we need to have a copy."

Maggie nodded in agreement and Mary Lou took the

paper to a copy machine in the corner. While she ran the copy, Maggie tried to look anywhere but at Ruth. She couldn't shake the feeling that in Ruth's eyes she was desecrating the historical society and everything for which it stood.

She glanced at the ceiling, then the floor, then the wall. She could hear the copy machine warming up and she wondered how long this was going to take exactly.

"I heard of him once," Ruth said.

"Excuse me?" Maggie said.

"I heard of Jasper Kasey but just once," Ruth said.

Maggie waited for her to say more. She didn't want Ruth to close up on her again, and she was afraid if she asked any questions, Ruth would stop talking.

"It was at a church social and I heard some of the ladies talking about Ida Dixon and why she had never married," Ruth said. "They said the love of her life Jasper Kasey left her at the altar, which I thought was sad. She was such a pretty lady."

Maggie said nothing, hoping Ruth would say more but she didn't. Mary Lou returned with the original document that she'd put in a manila folder.

"I promise I'll take very good care of it," she said.

Ruth looked like she wanted to say something but she remained silent. Mary Lou nodded, letting Maggie know it was okay for her to go.

When the door swung shut behind her, she could have sworn she felt the eyes of the two ladies on her back as she walked down the sidewalk to the police station.

She hoped she wasn't making too big of a deal about the list but her instincts told her that she wasn't, that this was important and that she had to show it to Sam.

She found him in his office. The station was quiet since it was so early in the morning. Given that they had just had breakfast together a little over an hour ago, Maggie was surprised that she felt her heart do that little tap dance thing it did every time she saw him. Maybe it was the white shirt and tie he had on, maybe it was the clean shaven jaw or maybe it was the fact that he was going to be her husband in just a few weeks.

That thought instantly squashed the pitter-patter of her heart with a tsunami of anxiety. She still didn't have a dress or a venue. Gah, she was the worst bride ever!

"Darling, you went from a giddy grin to a thunder-cloud frown in the blink of an eye," Sam said as he rose to his feet. "You all right?"

"I've been better," she said.

"Is it wedding jitters or Captain Bones or both?"

"Both," she said. "How'd you know?"

"I can read you like a book," he said. "Besides I've been feeling the same way."

Maggie raised her eyebrows.

"Well, not the wedding jitters part," he said. "I feel like we have that nailed."

"Having the pastor on speed dial does not mean we have it nailed," she said.

Sam grinned at her. "You're cute when you're nervous." When she didn't smile back, he grew serious. "Coffee?"

"That'd be great," she said.

"Sit tight," he said. "I'll be right back."

Maggie glanced at the clock on the wall. She had to get to her shop. The Good Buy Girls were coming around to discuss the wedding again. Suddenly, elopement didn't seem like such a bad idea, except for the wee detail about her mother never forgiving her.

"Here you go." Sam reentered the office with a mug in hand. He put it on the desk beside Maggie and paused to kiss the top of her head.

"So, talk to me," he said. "What's going on in that pretty head of yours?"

Maggie fortified herself with a sip of coffee before she spoke.

"I returned my books to the historical society today," she said.

Sam took his seat behind his desk. "You said you were going to do that. How'd it go? Was Ruth there?"

He made a comically alarmed face and Maggie knew that he shared her impression of Ruth being wrapped a bit too tight.

"Not at first," she said. "Mary Lou was there and she gave me a list of all of the men from the St. Stanley area who served in World War Two. I wanted to see if Jasper Kasey was listed and if so, did they have any biographical information on him?"

"Great idea," he said.

"I thought so," she said. She handed him the manila folder. "The list is in there. Now tell me if you think there is something odd going on."

Sam opened the folder and scanned the list. "The place where his name would fall alphabetically is covered up."

Maggie nodded. "It's too much of a coincidence, don't you think?"

Sam studied the list some more and then glanced up at her. When his blue eyes met hers, they were dark and determined.

"Way too much of a coincidence," he said.

Chapter 22

Maggie watched while Sam made a phone call. She could tell it was Andy he was talking to and not just because he greeted her by name but because there was a familiarity in his tone that he didn't use with everyone.

He explained about the paper and asked her to come and have a look at it. Then he got a perplexed look on his face and Maggie got the distinct impression he was uncomfortable. He hung up, looking distracted.

"Well, I'd better go open up the shop," Maggie said.

Sam nodded and then looked thoughtful. "I wonder if Andy is missing Richmond. I had to pull some strings to get her on loan to us but she seems really fixated on the old days."

Maggie made a noncommittal humming noise. She

knew this was the perfect opportunity to let Sam know what Andy had said to her about bringing him back to Richmond, but she held her tongue. She trusted Sam to make the right decision, really she did. More importantly, she wanted him to make the right decision for himself.

She gave him a quick kiss and dashed out the door right as his phone began to ring.

"So, do you think he finally gets that she wants him to return to the force in Richmond?" Ginger asked.

The Good Buy Girls met every week to swap coupons and share any online ads or circulars from the paper that they thought might help someone in the group. Usually, they met at Maggie's house but since her mother and sister were staying there, they had decided to meet for lunch at the Daily Grind. Summer had joined them, which was still odd for Maggie, but she was trying to rally.

"I don't know if he sees it that clearly yet, but I have hope for him," Maggie said.

"You're an id—" Summer began but then interrupted herself. "Sorry, old habits."

The rest of the Good Buy Girls looked at her and she shook her blond hair out as if shaking off her old miserable personality.

"What I meant to say was you are too trusting," Summer said. "There, that sounds better, doesn't it? You're about to marry this man. You do not need some old colleague from his past getting his head all spun around about where he wants to be. He belongs here with you and if you need to tattoo that onto the woman's forehead with your boot heel, I say do it."

"She has a point," Joanne said. Baby Patience was asleep in her stroller beside her and Joanne had taken the opportunity to eat a whole lunch: sandwich, iced tea and chips. Maggie had the feeling it wasn't always the norm for the busy new mother. Through a mouthful, Joanne added, "Boundaries have to be maintained."

Claire nodded. "I know if she was trying to get Pete to leave town, I'd want to kick her caboose all the way back to Richmond."

Ginger hooted. "Listen to all of this tough girl talk."

"Oh, come on, you know you'd put a beat down on her if she tried to get Roger to ditch you for his career," Summer said.

"Roger comes with four teenage boys," Ginger said. "No woman in her right mind would poach him for a career or a relationship because I would make sure the boys went with him."

"Clever," Maggie said. "So, can I borrow the boys?"

Ginger laughed. "I would not do that to you no matter how much they adore their Aunt Maggie."

"Like I said, I think Sam is figuring this out on his own. He just needs a little more time," Maggie said.

"If you say so," Summer said. "Just remember you have a wedding coming up, and if there is anything that will make a man bail in a blind panic that is it."

"Is that what you call positive talk?" Ginger asked.

"What?" Summer shrugged. She picked the tomatoes off of her sandwich before she took a bite. She swallowed and then said, "It is not helping that you don't have any of your wedding stuff in order. I don't think that sends a very good message to a groom."

To Maggie's surprise, all of the Good Buy Girls looked at her and not in support but as if they agreed with Summer's assessment of the situation.

"I have made some decisions," Maggie said.

"Do tell," Ginger said.

"Well, after some research, I discovered that buying flowers from a local grower is a lot more cost effective than having a florist make a ton of arrangements."

"And you've talked to a flower farmer to see what he's carrying?"

"It's on my to-do list," Maggie said. "Jim Peters has a peony farm and I was hoping to get him to sell them to me wholesale."

"He happens to be a client of mine," Ginger said. "I'll ask him. Your timing is good because I know his flowers are just beginning to bloom."

"Have a dress yet?" Summer asked.

"Working on it," Maggie said.

"How about a venue?" Claire asked.

"Again, working on it," Maggie said.

"Oh my god, you didn't book a venue yet. I'm going to start having a freak-out," Joanne said.

"No, no, it's all fine," Maggie lied. "Really, Sam said as long we have the pastor and the license he doesn't care about anything else."

"Oh, that's so romantic," Claire said. She sighed and Maggie wondered if she'd been on a Jane Austen bender lately. It had been known to happen.

The others nodded in agreement except for Summer, who rolled her eyes. Maggie had a feeling it was taking every bit of restraint Summer had not to give her a hard time.

"Well, there are some other ideas for affordable weddings," Ginger said. "For example, you could always have the wedding reception at your new house."

"The haunted house?" Summer asked. "You want to have a party in a haunted house?"

"Well, it's not necessarily a bad idea," Claire said. "According to my research, 81% of all wedding guests ranked the entertainment as the most memorable part of the wedding."

"Entertainment?" Maggie asked.

"And you can't get much more entertaining than ghosts," Ginger said.

Maggie lowered her head into her hands. Moving, skeletons, wedding, ghosts: She was going to have a nervous breakdown.

"Hey, I know," Claire said. "Pete knows a local cover band that plays in the coffee shop every now and then. They can play anything. I'll ask him to see if they're available. They all have jobs and mostly perform for fun. I heard one of them say they were just happy to play and even took payment in buffalo chicken wings once."

Maggie's head popped up. "Book 'em."

Claire grinned. "On it."

"See?" Ginger said. "It's all coming together."

"Unless Andy has her way," Summer said.

"What do you mean?" Maggie asked.

"Let me put it like this," Summer said. "If I were a betting woman, I'd lay odds that she was the one who strung that fishing line across the top step."

"But why?" Maggie said. She had told the girls earlier about the fishing line incident, but she had tried to play it off like it was a prank by some neighborhood kids. She didn't want anyone to worry unnecessarily. "Me being hurt doesn't help her get Sam back to Richmond."

"Unless you broke your neck," Summer said. "Then what reason would he have to stay?"

Maggie didn't like the way her heart clutched at that statement. She also wasn't thrilled that Summer had had the same thought she'd had about Andy. She was willing to let Summer try to be one of the Good Buy Girls but she was becoming increasingly uncomfortable with the realization that she and Summer seemed to think alike. It was disturbing.

"She's right. You're going to have to be careful until you know who might have done such a thing," Joanne said. She leaned over the stroller to check on Patience, who was still fast asleep.

"No going to the house by yourself," Claire said. "I can always come with you when I'm out of work."

"Same here," Ginger said. Maggie could tell by the pained expression on her face that of all the Good Buy Girls, she was the most afraid of the house. It was a testament to their friendship that she was willing to go in at all.

"Thank you," Maggie said. "I will be careful, but I still believe it was just a neighborhood kid playing a prank."

All four of them stared at her and she sighed.

"Or not."

Chapter 23

"So, I've been told that my lack of decisiveness about our wedding is a bad signal to you."

"In what way?" Sam asked.

Maggie and Sam had escaped their families and were enjoying a romantic dinner for two—well, along with Marshall Dillon—in their new home. Sam had brought a card table and folding chairs and they ate their take-out dinner from House of Noodles right out of the boxes.

"Well, it was theorized that you might think I don't want to get married to you," Maggie said. "But I just want you to know that I do and I've even made some decisions."

Sam grinned at her. "Okay, fire 'em at me."

"Peonies for flowers," she said. "All different colors.

I know we talked about calla lilies but I found a sweet deal on locally grown peonies."

"I'm okay with that. I think my grandmother grew those in her garden. Big round-headed things, aren't they? I always liked those."

"Good," she said.

"And Claire has a cover band contact through Pete for a really talented group of musicians that I hear will work for chicken wings," she said.

Sam bit into his egg roll. "How about a roasted pig?"

Maggie tipped her head to the side. "Huh?"

"Michael and I were thinking a big old luau-style roast pig would be the ticket for food," he said.

"This means I don't have to find a caterer?" Maggie asked.

Sam nodded. "I'll take care of the food."

"I love it," Maggie said. "Now as to where we should have the reception—"

"Here," Sam interrupted her. "I think it should be here."

Maggie grinned. "I was thinking the same thing."

Sam's phone buzzed. He glanced at it but didn't answer it.

"Let's move in after the wedding, that way we don't have to do anything but rent tables and chairs and put a roasting pit in the backyard," Sam said.

Maggie let out a very uncharacteristic squeal which made Sam laugh. She reached across the table and squeezed his hand.

"I think we have a wedding," she said.

Sam's phone buzzed again. He glanced at it and she could tell by the way his lips tightened he was unhappy at the interruption.

"What about invitations?" he asked.

"Meh, in a town this size, let's just invite everyone," Maggie said.

"It's not likely that they'll misbehave at the sheriff's house," Sam said. "All right, everyone it is."

"I'm sure I can ask Bianca Madison to get the word out," Maggie said. "She has that annual ball every year and she manages to invite everyone."

"See, it's all coming together," Sam said. "I never had any doubt that you wanted this. Only that you were a bit overwhelmed with so much change so fast."

"I was, but I think I'm feeling better," Maggie said. "And hey, we've been here for over an hour and there's been no sign of any ghostly activity."

As soon as she said it they both glanced around the room, but there was nothing. Instead, Sam's phone started buzzing again, making Maggie jump.

"I think you need to answer it," she said. "Whoever it is, they're very persistent."

"It's Andy," he said. He frowned and then answered, "Collins."

"Uh-huh," he said. "No, I can't come over to the ME's right now."

Maggie took an egg roll out of their shared carton and nibbled on it while she blatantly listened to the conversation.

"I'm sure it is fascinating," Sam said. "But unless there

is a reason you can't give me the information over the phone, I'd like you to just tell me now."

Maggie glanced away. She had only heard Sam's voice get this short when he was very irritated.

"Thank you for confirming the identity of the skeleton," he said. "And how about the paper?"

Sam tapped his chopsticks against the carton while he listened. Maggie wished she could hear what was being said, but she knew he'd tell her as soon as he hung up.

"Thank you, Andy, you've done a great job here," he said. He glanced at Maggie and then said, "I think you're good to head back to Richmond now."

Maggie could hear very excited chatter on the other end of the phone, although she couldn't make out the words.

"No, I really think it's for the best," Sam said. "But again, thank you and nice work."

He ended the call while Andy was still talking.

"Did you just hang up on her?" Maggie asked. Rudeness was not generally Sam's way.

"There's something I need to tell you," he said.

Maggie put down her carton of food. Oh, boy, was this it? Had Sam finally figured out Andy's game? And if he had, how did he feel about it? He sounded irritated with her but maybe it was because Andy had struck a nerve. Maybe he did want to go back to Richmond, or even worse, maybe he wanted to go back and he wanted Maggie to go with him, where she'd be forced to spend more time with Andy. Gah! It was completely unacceptable. She forced herself to breathe. No sense in panicking until she heard what he had to say. Right? Right.

"Last night while I was on duty, Andy showed up at the station," he said. "She was drunk."

Maggie raised her eyebrows. She hadn't pegged Andy as a drinker.

"Andy is having a hard time back in Richmond," he said. "A lot of the old guard, like me, has retired and she's not working so well with the new powers that be."

"Is that why she wants you to come back?" Maggie asked.

"You knew?" Sam looked surprised.

"She told me when she first got here that her plan was to bring you back to Richmond and I could either pack a bag and come with or kiss you good-bye," she said.

"And you never said anything to me?" he asked.

"I wanted you to make up your own mind," she said.

"Maggie O'Brien Gerber soon-to-be Collins, you never cease to amaze me," he said. "You do know there was never any question of me going back?"

"I do now," she said.

He kissed her on the mouth and Maggie forgot where she was and what she was supposed to be doing. Sam Collins had been turning her brain to mush since he'd first kissed her in a back alley over twenty years ago. She knew now that was never going to change, and she welcomed it.

"There's one more thing you should know about last night," Sam said when he pulled away.

Maggie shook her head in an effort to focus. "What's that?"

"As I was pouring coffee down Andy's throat and

listening to her tale of woe while insisting that there was no way I was going back to Richmond, I had two visitors."

"Who?" Maggie asked.

"Summer and Tyler Fawkes," he said.

"Now I'm lost," Maggie said. "Why would they have popped in on you?"

"Because Summer was tailing Andy, thinking that she was up to no good, which she was," he said.

"Whoa, whoa, whoa," Maggie cried as she hopped up from her seat. "Stop the crazy train. Are you telling me that Summer had my back?"

"Yup," Sam said.

Maggie stared at him. "I can't . . . that's impossible . . . I'm not sure I can process this."

"Tell me about it," Sam said. "Summer looked like she was going to put a hurt on Andy, and I think only Tyler holding her back kept her from doing so."

"That's crazy," Maggie said.

"No, that's loyalty," he said. He cleared his throat and said, "It makes you wonder."

"Wonder if Summer has gone round the bend?" she asked.

"No, it makes you wonder how far someone will go to protect someone they love."

"What do you mean?"

"I've been reading up on the Dixon family," he said. "That book Ruth lent you that you forgot to return, and I was struck by the thought that if you read between the lines, Ida was a bit of a handful for Imogene."

"Yes, I got that, too. It seemed as if their father had a hard time raising Imogene and Ida on his own," Maggie said. "But they were both very active in the community and really did a lot of good works."

"And yet, there was a dead man in their root cellar," Sam said.

"What are you thinking?"

Sam dug in his carton with his chop sticks. He popped a bite of sweet-and-sour chicken into his mouth and chewed as if gathering his thoughts before he spoke.

"Maybe Ida got into trouble with Jasper and Imogene took care of the problem," he said.

They were both silent as if waiting for the house—or more accurately a spirit in the house—to slam a door or flick the lights on and off. There was nothing.

"Or maybe Imogene was afraid Ida would get married and leave her," Maggie said.

Again, they both waited but there was nothing.

Sam let out a long sigh. "I can't believe I'm actually throwing out theories and hoping the house will give me a clue."

Maggie sat back down and gave him a sheepish smile. "Me, too."

"You know, I just don't see the sisters living here if they knew there was a body in their basement," Sam said. "I didn't get the crazy vibe from their bios. Eccentric, yes, crazy, no."

"So, you think someone else killed Jasper Kasey and the sisters never knew," Maggie said.

Bam! A door slammed upstairs and the lights flickered overhead.

"Ah!" Maggie yelped and Sam started. Marshall Dillon came racing across the room with his tail at full fluff.

When Maggie's heart stopped racing, she looked at Sam. "Do you think that was a 'By George, I think they've got it!' door slam?"

Sam gave her a wide-eyed look. "With a 'Finally!' light flicker? Yes, I do."

"Who would know for sure?" Maggie asked.

They looked at each other and said at the same time, "Ruth Crenshaw."

Chapter 24

As she stepped into the small building once again, Maggie realized that she had been in the St. Stanley Historical Society more in the past week than she had in her entire life.

Mary Lou Sutton was behind the desk. There was no sign of Ruth. Maggie wasn't sure if she was relieved or not. She knew Sam was going to be coming by to interview Ruth and that she really needed to butt out, but on her way to work her curiosity had gotten the better of her. Besides she had to return the book she had forgotten. She could admit that she was a little afraid of Ruth and didn't want the woman coming after her for the book.

"Hi, Mary Lou," Maggie greeted the woman behind the desk.

"Maggie, thank goodness," Mary Lou said.

Maggie looked at her in surprise. She held out the book in her hand and said, "I'm sorry this is late."

Mary Lou took the book. "No, it's just that I'm here alone and I really need to use the bathroom, but I didn't want to lock up and hear it from Ruth about abandoning my post."

"Ruth isn't in today?" she asked.

"No," Mary Lou said. She sounded annoyed. "Not yet anyway. Do you mind keeping an eye while I go—"

Maggie waved her hand. "Not at all. Go."

Mary Lou flashed a grateful smile. "I'll be quick."

"No problem. Do you think Ruth is all right?" Maggie asked.

"Who knows?" Mary Lou shrugged. "You know when I took this job a few months ago, I thought I would have proper training. Instead, I just get put on endless tasks like digitizing the files. She never lets me do any of the research."

"Ruth has been running this place a long time by herself," Maggie said. "Maybe giving up control is hard for her."

"That's not it," Mary Lou said. She glanced around the room as if someone might have appeared who could overhear them. "She's been odd ever since you and Sheriff Collins bought up the Dixon house."

"Odd how?" Maggie asked.

"Nervous, twitchy," Mary Lou said. "It's like she has something to hide. It's just weird."

She disappeared through the door, leaving Maggie to puzzle out her words. What could Ruth be nervous about?

Was it Sam's questioning her about the Dixon house? Did she know more than she was saying? Maggie wandered around the room. She browsed the shelves, looking at the historical volumes that covered the town, the county, the state and even the country.

It never ceased to amaze her that St. Stanley was just a stepping-off place for many of its residents. They'd had a United States senator, a rock band and a soap opera star all come from this tiny town nestled in the Virginia hills.

Maggie wondered if her life might have played out differently if she had left St. Stanley. She had assumed when she'd married Charlie that he would work his way up to sheriff in some other town and had always figured that they would move, but when he was killed, she had pulled her community into her heart to help buffer the pain and the fear of being on her own. The people of St. Stanley hadn't let her down and now she could never imagine living anywhere else.

Mary Lou arrived back in the room, breaking Maggie out of her reverie.

"Thanks so much." Mary Lou let out a breath. "I think I can make it now."

"Good," Maggie said. "You know, if Ruth doesn't turn up, you may want to call Sheriff Collins."

Mary Lou nodded. "I'm sure she's fine. She's just working through something."

Maggie tipped her head to the side and studied the other woman. "Mary Lou, is there something you're not telling me?"

Mary Lou bit her lip and then the words burst out of her in a gust of air. "You can't tell anyone about this."

"Okay."

Mary Lou glanced around the room as if to make sure they were still alone. "I did some reading in the restricted books."

"Restricted books?" Maggie asked.

"Shh," Mary Lou hushed her and they both leaned forward over the counter. Mary Lou continued in a whisper, "Those are the books she keeps upstairs that no one is allowed to touch because they're fragile."

"Oh." Maggie nodded.

"One of the books is her mother Violet Crenshaw's diary," Mary Lou said.

She reached below the counter and pulled out a small, red, leather-bound book. The edges were worn and the binding was cracked and Maggie could see that the pages were yellowed. There was no question it was an old book. Mary Lou pushed the book at Maggie.

"I think the answers you're looking for are in there but if you tell anyone, especially Ruth, where you got the information, I'll deny it. Also, you have to get the book back to me as soon as possible, preferably before she notices that it's gone."

Maggie quickly tucked the book into her purse. "Thank you, Mary Lou."

Mary Lou made a shooing gesture with her hands. "It's fine but go before she gets here and remember: Do not say a word."

"My lips are sealed," Maggie said and she hurried out the door.

She had parked behind the small building and as she hurried to her car, she noted that her car looked oddly lopsided. She moved closer and realized that her right front tire was flat.

Maggie glanced at her watch. She'd have to call Sal from the garage to come and fix her flat. She did not have time for this. She had to be at the shop and ready to open in fifteen minutes, which was about how long it would take her to walk there.

She made sure her car was locked and then hurried up the sidewalk to the main road. She knew she could take a shortcut along one of the neighborhood streets and get to the back of her shop in less time.

She felt like a felon fleeing down the street with the Crenshaw diary in her bag. She'd had no idea there was a restricted collection of books in the historical society and she was betting no one else did either. As soon as she got to the shop, she planned to call Claire and see if she knew about it.

She knew Ruth was an odd duck, and Mary Lou's report about Ruth behaving strangely made Maggie uneasy. Could the person who tied the trip wire to the porch steps the night that Maggie fell be Ruth? The idea boggled.

Lost in thought and with the Crenshaw diary burning a hole in her purse, Maggie took a sharp turn down the narrow tree-lined residential street, planning to jaywalk halfway down to get to her shop.

She paused to look both ways before stepping into the road. She took three steps when a small dark-green sedan came screeching around the corner headed right for her. Maggie had heard the saying that your life flashes before your eyes when you stare impending death right in the kisser, but it wasn't true.

She got nothing, nada, bubkes. There was no remembering her first kiss, birthing her daughter or reconnecting with Sam. Her brain instead made a loud buzzing noise like an entire swarm of bees were encircling her head, and she couldn't think through the hum enough to tell her legs to move.

The car was right on top of her when some crazy instinct kicked in, and she leapt back onto the sidewalk in an ungraceful frog hop that caused her to go splat while the sedan zoomed away, disappearing around the next corner.

"Crazy drivers!" a crotchety voice shouted from a nearby yard.

Old Man Hanley was standing in his yard holding his hose over his rose bushes in one hand while he shook his other fist in the direction of the car.

"Don't just stand there cursing, George," the kinder, gentler Mrs. Hanley chided him. "Help Maggie up."

Mr. Hanley dropped his hose and came at a fast shuffle to Maggie's side.

"Are you all right?" he asked. "Do you need me to call Doc Franklin?"

Maggie got to her feet, feeling her knees knocking against each other as she did. There was a tear in her jeans at the knee and she could feel a little blood gushing out of the wound, but otherwise she was fine. Heck, she was alive so she was great.

"I think my dignity took the hardest hit," she said.

Old Man Hanley clapped her on the shoulder. "That's what I've always liked about you, Maggie. You've got spirit."

"Come on in and get cleaned up, dear," Mrs. Hanley said.

Where Mr. Hanley was big and rawboned, Mrs. Hanley had the delicate build of a sparrow. Glancing between them, Maggie had a feeling the sparrow ruled the birdhouse.

"Thanks, but I have to open my shop," Maggie said. "I can clean up there."

"Oh, are you sure?" Mrs. Hanley asked. "That's a nasty scrape."

"Yes, I'm fine, really," Maggie said. "Besides I want to call the sheriff and report that driver."

Old Man Hanley nodded in approval. "That's right, sic your boyfriend on them. That'll teach them."

Maggie smiled and began to walk away. Her knee was stiff but she figured it was probably better to be moving it, even if she did feel the blood dripping down into her shoe.

While she walked she took out her phone and called Sam. Not, as Mr. Hanley had suggested, to sic her boyfriend on the driver but rather because she recognized the green sedan. She remembered it from where it was always parked in front of the historical society. It belonged to Ruth Crenshaw.

Chapter 25

By the time Maggie arrived at her shop, she found Ginger pacing at the back door.

Before she could say a word, Ginger hugged her tight and said, "Sam called me. He's out looking for the car and told me to come and make sure you're all right."

"I'm fine," Maggie said. And this time when she said it, she meant it.

"You could have been killed," Ginger said. "I am in no way prepared to lose my best friend."

"You're not going to lose me," Maggie said. She unlocked the back door and let them both in.

"I'll make coffee," Ginger said. "You go clean that knee."

Maggie went into the bathroom. She opened the

cabinet and retrieved ointment and bandages. She washed the cut out with soap and water, which stung to no end, and while it air dried, she opened her purse to check on the state of the book.

She hadn't thought of it until now, but if anything had happened to the Crenshaw diary, she would have felt horrible. Thankfully, it was as intact as it had been when Mary Lou gave it to her.

Unable to resist, Maggie cracked the volume open and began to peruse the pages. She flipped through Violet Crenshaw's entries, although she was Violet Minton in the beginning of the diary as she had yet to meet Craig Crenshaw, her future husband.

She kept very detailed descriptions of the events she attended and the Sunday school classes she taught. She had a wry humor that made Maggie smile. She had flipped through a quarter of the volume before a name leapt out at her. Jasper Kasey!

Maggie devoured the next few pages, forgetting all about her throbbing knee, her near-death experience and the fact that she was holed up in a bathroom. Ruth had told her that she had only heard Jasper Kasey's name mentioned once, but if her own mother had been engaged to him that had to be a lie. Why would Ruth lie?

She read about Violet's love story with Jasper Kasey. According to the diary, Jasper swept her off her feet and they were engaged shortly after they first met.

Ruth had never mentioned her mother's relationship with Jasper Kasey. Why not? Maggie flipped ahead in the diary and it was then that she noticed several pages had been torn from it. In fact a whole section was missing. Could that be the evidence Sam needed to determine who had killed Jasper Kasey and stuffed him in the Dixon basement?

An insistent knocking on the door broke her concentration and Ginger called out, "What happened? Did you fall in?"

Maggie started and hastily shoved the diary back into her purse. She opened the door and found Ginger standing there, looking worried.

"I need to talk to Sam," she said.

Ginger looked her up and down. "Didn't you go in there to put a bandage on?"

"I forgot," Maggie said.

"Forgot?" Summer asked as she appeared behind Ginger. "You're bleeding all over your jeans and you forgot? Did you hit your head when you fell?"

"What's she doing here?" Maggie asked Ginger.

"All of the Good Buy Girls are here," Ginger said. "Come on, let's go out front. You can make your call while I bandage your knee myself."

Sure enough Claire and Joanne with baby Patience were sitting out front waiting for her. When she arrived with Ginger and Summer, they both jumped to their feet and began firing questions.

"What happened?"

"Are you all right?"

"Do you know who did this?"

"Give the woman a chance to catch her breath," Summer said. "And I think it's pretty clear who did this."

"It is?" Maggie asked. She couldn't fathom how Summer could know about Ruth.

"Yes, it's that Andy woman," she said. "Clearly, she hasn't given up on bringing Sam back to Richmond."

"No!" Claire said. She looked shocked.

"But she works for the police," Joanne protested.

"That doesn't mean she doesn't do bad things," Summer said.

"She has a point," Ginger said. "That woman was pretty determined to bring Sam back to his old life."

"But trying to kill me just so she could have her work buddy back seems a little above and beyond crazy," Maggie said. "No, I think it was—"

The door to the shop opened with a clang of bells and Maggie stopped in mid-sentence as she took in the sight of her mother walking in with Sam's mother. Neither of them looked very happy. That was an understatement. They were glaring daggers at each other.

"Tell this woman that she is not allowed to make decisions regarding your wedding cake," Maggie's mother said. She crossed her arms over her chest and glared at Sam's mother.

"Uh-oh," Ginger said under her breath.

"What do you mean 'uh-oh'?" Summer asked. "This is fixing to be good."

Maggie frowned at her and Summer sighed. "Sorry."

"Well, given that my opinion of the flowers didn't matter, I just thought I would help in some small way." Trudy Collins sniffed. "Clearly my help isn't wanted."

"No, it's not that," Maggie protested. "It's just that

there's been so much going on, but you don't need to worry. Sam and I have everything under control."

"Really?" Lizzie turned to look at her daughter. "Do tell."

"Sit," Ginger said to Maggie. "You can talk while I get this bandage on you."

"Bandage?" Trudy Collins asked. "What happened to your knee?"

"She was almost ru—" Summer began but Maggie interrupted.

"I fell," Maggie said. She gave Summer a look and Summer shrugged as if to say lying is pointless because they're going to find out anyway. That was fine with Maggie so long as they figured it out when they weren't with her and couldn't fuss her into suffocation.

"That is a nasty scrape," Lizzie said.

"Your dress should cover it though, right?" Trudy asked. She leaned over Maggie to examine her knee and Maggie felt as if she were under a laser-like scrutiny that would determine whether she was lying or not. Given that Sam was one of four boys, she was pretty sure Trudy Collins had perfected the look.

"Yes, absolutely," Maggie said.

"You have your dress?" Lizzie asked.

Ginger chose that moment to hit Maggie's scrape with an antiseptic wipe and Maggie about leapt out of her chair.

"Ow, ow, ow, ow!" she yelped.

"Sorry, but timing is everything," Ginger said.

Maggie met her gaze and knew that her friend had

just saved her from confessing that she didn't have a dress yet. That's what best friends were for.

"What about a venue?" Trudy was clearly not going to be deterred from discussing wedding details even by a little blood.

"They are not using the banquet hall at your country club," Lizzie said.

"Well, I refuse to see my son get married in the great room at your favorite restaurant," Trudy argued.

They were both getting a little red and blotchy, and Maggie was afraid that things were going to go from bad to worse at any moment.

"No, no," she said. "You don't have to worry. Sam and I have agreed to have the reception at the new house."

"That's right," Joanne said. "And my husband is providing the pig for roasting."

"And my boyfriend has a cover band all lined up for entertainment," Claire said.

"And my husband is getting all of the tables and chairs," Summer said.

"Does he know this?" Ginger asked.

"Not yet, but he will," Summer said. "I didn't want to be left out."

"Me neither," Ginger agreed. "That's why I'm taking care of the cake, which will be chocolate with vanilla buttercream and decorated with a cascade of peonies going around the side, right?"

"Yes. Really? You are?" Maggie asked.

"Absolutely," Ginger said. "I'm pretty sure I can get help from Alice Franklin with the frosting part of it."

"She is gifted in the frosting arts," Claire said.

"See?" Maggie looked at the two mothers. "It's all taken care of so you have nothing to worry about."

"Nothing to worry about?" Lizzie squawked. "This is a travesty!"

"A fiasco," Trudy agreed.

"You can't have a wedding reception in a haunted house," Lizzie said. "You shouldn't even be planning to live there. How can your guests possibly expect to relax when they'll be looking over their shoulders for ghosts the entire time?"

"She's right," Trudy said. "It's a horrible idea. No doubt my son put her up to it."

"Oh, Sam wasn't alone in this half-baked idea. Some of the things Maggie has cooked up over the years, honestly, is it any wonder that my hair is gray?"

"Oh, please, you are a lovely mother of the bride," Trudy said. "Look at all of this salt and pepper. When they first started sprouting, I used to name them after each boy who caused me a fright. I could point to my head and say, 'Tommy, Jake, Nate, Sam, Sam, Sam, Sam.'"

Lizzie O'Brien covered her mouth while she giggled and Maggie stared at the two women, who had entered enemies and were now leaving as friends.

"I think they might just be a perfect match," Lizzie said. Both women turned to look at Maggie with matching expressions of adoration.

"Still, we'd better get moving on the decoration portion of this shindig, before it gets forgotten," Trudy said. "I think peach linens would be lovely."

"Yes, we could do that, or maybe a nice royal blue," Lizzie said.

They turned and began to leave the shop, not even bothering to say good-bye to anyone.

"How about royal blue with peach accents?" Trudy asked.

"I like it," Lizzie said.

The door swung shut behind them and Maggie leaned back against her seat and closed her eyes.

"What was that?" she asked.

"Turbo mothers of the bride and groom," Summer said. "They are the reason some people elope."

"Speaking of turbo mothers, how is Blair?" Claire asked.

"Still mad at me for eloping," Summer said. Then she grinned. "That was months ago and she still isn't speaking to me, which is a nice vacation from her constant criticism."

"But she and Tyler are getting along?" Joanne asked.

"Ever since he saved her life and she found out he was loaded—okay, mostly after she found out he was loaded—he is her favorite person," Summer sighed.

"Maybe she'll meet someone soon," Ginger said.

"You may want to trot her over to Spring Gardens," Maggie said. "I know that both Dennis Applebaum and his brother are on the prowl and they could certainly use a firm hand from a strong-willed woman; also I heard that they're quite well off."

"Hmm." Summer narrowed her gaze at Maggie. "Are you helping me out?"

"Maybe," Maggie said. "Because I heard that friends do that sort of thing for each other, you know, like looking out for someone's fiancé when someone is trying to break them up."

Summer's eyes went wide. "Did Sam tell you? I told him not to tell you."

"Yeah, he did," Maggie said. "And I'm glad. That was a nice thing you did and I appreciate it."

Summer ducked her head and her hair covered her face. Maggie couldn't tell if she was embarrassed or suddenly shy, having never seen Summer exhibit either of those emotions before.

"I'm lost," Ginger said. "Catch me up to speed, please."

Maggie told the rest of the Good Buy Girls what Sam had told her about Summer tailing Andy and keeping an eye on her. They all looked as amazed as Maggie had felt at the time.

"You know, I had my doubts about you, Summer, but I have to say you are certainly proving yourself worthy of the Good Buy Girl membership," Ginger said.

"I can go one better than that," Summer said. She glanced up and Maggie noted that her cheeks were pink with embarrassment. "I talked to Tyler about using one of his investments for your weddings favors, because I noticed you hadn't really come up with one yet."

Maggie felt her smile freeze. Given that Summer's style was a bit more flamboyant than Maggie's—as in a bit more slutty—she was afraid to find out what sort of investment would yield favors for her wedding.

"Here, I'll show you," Summer said. She reached into

her voluminous handbag and pulled out a cube-shaped box. She popped the top and lifted out a clear ball-shaped glass jar with a cork for a stopper and a small wooden honey dipper tied to its neck. The jar was filled with a pretty amber liquid.

Summer held it out to her. "It's a jar of honey from Tyler's beekeeper business. I figured we could tie on a tag with your names and the date and use them as favors. I mean everyone likes honey, right?"

Maggie took the jar and felt her throat get tight. If anyone had told her that there would be a day where she felt compelled to hug Summer and not in a choke-her-out sort of way, she would have thought they were crazy.

She glanced up at the woman who had been a thorn in her side since she first sucked air. Then she stepped close and hugged her.

"It's perfect," Maggie said. "Thank you."

After an awkward second, Summer hugged her back. "You're welcome."

When they broke apart, they gave each other sheepish grins.

"That is absolutely perfect, Summer," Joanne said. She gave her a hug and Ginger did the same. Claire, not being a hugger by nature, left it at a fist bump.

"Maggie, I don't want to jinx it but I can't help but think you are going to have the best wedding ever," Ginger said. Maggie didn't want to jinx it either so she said nothing, but just nodded, hoping that her silent agreement did not invite mayhem into one of the most important days of her life.

Chapter 26

When she thought about it, Maggie knew she didn't need the best wedding ever, she just needed a non-ghost infested event that would find her married to her first love Sam Collins at the end of it. She had to admit life sure was full of surprises. If someone had told her five years ago that this was how it was going to play out, she would have thought they were demented. Now she couldn't imagine her life going any other way.

Shortly after the mothers left the shop, the Good Buy Girls all left to carry on with their own days. It took some pushing, but Maggie convinced Ginger that she was fine. She had a call in to Sam as he was still out looking for Ruth.

She wanted to tell Sam about the diary but not over

the phone. And truthfully, she wanted to finish reading it before she turned it over to him.

Maggie figured as long as she stayed alert, she really didn't have to worry that Ruth was going to make another move to hurt her. After mulling over the incident, she knew that if Ruth had really wanted to kill her, she could have easily run Maggie over. It seemed she just wanted to scare Maggie, so in that regard, mission accomplished.

When Sam called to check on her, Maggie promised to keep her phone on her person at all times, which seemed to put him at ease. Maggie mentioned that she needed to talk to him, and he said he would be stopping by as soon as he finished running down the lead that Ruth's car was in the lot at the hospital.

While Maggie was ringing up a pretty sundress for Megan Pritchard, she felt her phone vibrate in her pocket. It was an incoming text from Tyler Fawkes. He wanted to know how many tables he should pick up for the wedding party at the house.

Maggie frowned. She had no idea. They texted back and forth until Maggie knew the size of the tables and how much room they would take up with chairs. She knew she was going to have to stop by the house and do some measuring before she could answer Tyler's question.

Wanting to get it done before she forgot, Maggie decided to stop by the house on her way home. As she closed and locked the shop door, she called Sam to let him know what she was doing.

"Hi, darling," Sam answered. "Are you all right?"

"I'm fine," Maggie assured him.

"How's the knee?"

"Better. Have you had any luck finding Ruth?"

"We found her car parked on her street, not at the hospital, but there was no sign of her," he said. He sounded grim. "I want you to be extremely careful until we do."

"I will, I promise," Maggie said. "I've been in touch with Tyler about the tables for the reception. I need to stop by the house and measure the main rooms to figure out how many we can fit in there."

"Don't we want to set up outside?" Sam asked.

"What if it rains?"

"We can put up big tents," he said.

"All right, but I still need to measure the backyard and figure out how we're going to lay it all out."

"I don't want you at the house by yourself," he said.

"So meet me," Maggie said. She thought about the diary, hating to give it up before she had read the whole thing, but still she knew it was the right thing to do. "I have something to give you."

"That sounds promising," Sam said.

"It's got to do with Jasper Kasey," Maggie said.

"Now I'm intrigued," he said. "I can be there in half an hour."

"Perfect," Maggie agreed. "I'll meet you on the front porch."

"Do not go into the house or the backyard without me," Sam said.

"I promise," Maggie said.

They ended their call with their usual *I love you*s and

Maggie put her phone back in her pocket. She had forgotten to call Sal at the garage, so she was going to have to walk across town to get to the house, which would take most of the half hour. She figured if she cut through the town green, she would be safe enough; besides if she got there early, she'd have a few minutes to look through the diary.

She locked up the shop and set out toward the center of town. She loved June. It was warm but not yet sticky with humidity. Hanging flower pots bursting with rainbows of vibrant petunias hung from the lampposts that lined the streets in the center of town. It was hard to feel afraid when the world was so fresh and green and full of beauty and optimism.

She thought about what she knew about Ruth Crenshaw. Always a bit odd, Ruth had worked at the historical society for as long as Maggie could remember. She had never married or had children. She had lived in her family home her whole life, staying to take care of her parents as they aged. As far as Maggie knew, an occasional shopping trip to Dumontville was as far as Ruth had ever ventured from home.

Could it be that Ruth's mother Violet held the key to what had happened to Jasper Kasey? They had been engaged and in the diary, she talked all about her plans for a big wedding and how exciting it was to be marrying a pilot. What had happened? Had Jasper thrown Violet over for Ida? Had she killed him and put his body in the Dixon house to frame Ida? Was that what had been written in the missing pages?

Did Ruth know what her mother had done and was she trying to hide it? Ruth's devotion to her parents might cause her to try and hide something shameful in their past, but it was hard for Maggie to believe that she would harm Maggie in the process. Then again, if her mother had killed her fiancé, the family could be prone to violent behavior.

Maggie left the town green and walked down the side street where her new home sat nestled amidst the other historic homes of St. Stanley. She liked this street. It was wide and lined with trees, the houses had big front yards and most had wrought iron or white picket fences. She thought about the garden she wanted to plant and the porch swing she planned to have installed. Spending her days here with Sam would be lovely, assuming they could evict their ghost and deal with Ruth.

Maggie walked up the gravel drive. She liked the sound of the crunch under her sneakers. A lilac bush in the corner of the yard was heavy with blooms and she could smell its sweet bouquet in the breeze. She paused, wondering if they could use the front yard for the wedding, but she doubted any of her new neighbors wanted a pig roast in their line of sight.

She climbed the steps to the porch, checking for a trip wire just in case. There was nothing, which made her shoulders fall back down from around her ears. She hadn't even realized she'd been that tense until she felt herself relax.

She checked the door. It was locked. She paced the length of the porch but nothing seemed amiss. Her phone buzzed and she looked at the display to see a text from Sam. He was running late but would be there in ten minutes.

Maggie sat back down and began to listen to the crickets. She glanced at the tall trees in the yard, anticipating a light show from the fireflies that seemed to enjoy flitting through the branches.

She remembered when her daughter used to catch jarfuls of the bugs and she'd let her keep them just until bedtime but then they always let them go. It had been magical to watch them fly back out into the world. She wondered if she would feel that same sense of freedom when Ruth was caught and her house was specter free.

She opened her purse and pulled Violet Crenshaw's diary from it. She had just a few minutes before it would be too dark to read. She knew she had told Sam she wouldn't go inside the house but surely putting on the porch light would be okay.

As she rose from her seat, she glanced along the side of the house and noticed a glow coming from one of the basement windows. That was odd. She was sure that Sam and the officers had shut everything off when they left the basement and as far as she knew he hadn't been back.

She walked over to the window just above the ground. She peered in through the dirty glass and her breath caught in her throat. There was a light on in the basement, but more importantly, she saw Ruth Crenshaw.

Ruth was sitting on the dirt floor with her hands and feet tied in front of her and a gag tied around her mouth.

Maggie didn't pause to think about what she was doing; she banged on the window, bringing Ruth's attention to her.

Ruth's eyes went wide and she shook her head wildly back and forth as if warning Maggie away. Maggie tried to pry open the window to let Ruth know she was coming, but she couldn't get the old painted frame to budge.

She pulled her phone out of her pocket and dialed Sam's number. He answered on the second ring.

"He—" he began but Maggie interrupted.

"Ruth, I found Ruth," she said. She stared at Ruth through the window as if afraid to take her eyes off of her for a second.

"What? Where?" Sam demanded. "Maggie, are you all right?"

"I'm fine. I'm at the house," Maggie said. "She's in the basement."

"Where are you exactly?" Sam demanded. Maggie heard a siren over the phone and knew that Sam was racing to get to her.

"Sam, she's tied up. Ah!" Maggie gasped as the lights in the basement went out. "The lights just went out. I'm going in."

"Maggie, you can't," Sam yelled. "You don't know what's happening."

"I know Ruth is tied up in the basement and it just went dark," Maggie yelled back. "I have to go in."

"Wait for me!" Sam said.

"What if she gets killed?" Maggie argued.

"She won't," Sam said.

Maggie could hear the doubt in his voice and she

knew he was thinking the same thing she was. She had to go in.

"I'll stay on the phone," Maggie said. She used her key to unlock the door and pushed it open.

"Maggie." Sam's voice was a low, growled warning.

Maggie ignored him. She listened to the house, trying to determine if anyone was near her. She couldn't hear anything.

"Ruth! Sam and I are here!" she shouted, hoping that whoever had tied Ruth up had heard her and opted to run rather than face her and phone Sam.

"Maggie, don't go in there," Sam said. He sounded frantic.

"I have to," Maggie whispered. "You know I do."

She heard him emit an anxious exhale on the other end in unspoken reluctant agreement.

Maggie stepped into the house, keeping close to the wall. She reached for the light switch that she knew was to her right. Her fingers had just found the switch when a loud *thwack* rang in her ears and a burst of pain exploded in the back of her head. Before Maggie could flip the switch and see who had hit her, she was out cold, falling to the floor in a heap.

Chapter 27

Pain, insistent, relentless, throbbing pain, roused
Maggie. She blinked and for a moment she was sure she'd
been blinded as complete darkness was all she could see.
But then, a faint line in front of her alluded to light and
she stared at it until her eyes adjusted and she could make
out the bottom of a door.

She sat up and stretched her legs out, but she hit a wall.
She reached out with her left hand and hit another wall.
She could feel another at her back and she knew she was
in a closet. But where? Was she at the house? She turned
her head and it throbbed, clearly resistant to being moved.

She reached out with her right hand, trying to feel in
the darkness for anything that would give her a clue as

to where she was. Her fingers closed around a scratchy fabric.

A muttered oath made her jump, making her head pound even harder. The scratchy fabric was on a body, but whose?

"Who are you?" Maggie demanded. She cringed against the throb in her temples.

A muffled answer made her realize that whoever it was was gagged. Ruth! She'd seen Ruth bound and gagged in the cellar. It had to be her.

"Hold on," Maggie said. "Let me untie you."

She felt around in the darkness until she found Ruth's head. She followed her hair until she found the knot for the gag, and she tried to untie it. It was difficult in the dark. Whoever had tightened the knots had done a heck of a job. Finally, Maggie got the gag loose enough to slip over Ruth's head.

"Ruth, is that you?" she asked.

"Yes." Ruth's voice wasn't much more than a rasp.

"Where are we? Who did this to you? Why are we bound in a closet?"

"Mary Lou," Ruth said.

"What? Is she in danger, too?" Maggie asked.

"No, it's her," Ruth said.

"Mary Lou did this?" Maggie gasped.

"Shh," Ruth hissed. In a whisper, she continued, "I don't know where she is."

"Do you know where we are?" Maggie whispered. "Are we in my house?"

"Sort of," Ruth said. "She dragged us into the tool shed

at the back of the property. I think this is some sort of closet. I hope there aren't any spiders. I hate spiders."

The cramped space did have a particular musty odor like mushrooms blended with cedar. Maggie thought it smelled familiar from the tour of the shed she and Sam had taken a few weeks ago.

"How did she get us here?" Maggie asked.

"She carried me and she dragged you," Ruth said. "I heard your fiancé roar up, but Mary Lou just shut and latched the door."

"Oh my god, Sam is going to go completely mental if he gets to the house and we're not there," Maggie said.

"Why would he care about me?" Ruth asked.

"Because when I saw you through the basement window, I called Sam to tell him you were tied up down there," Maggie said. "He was on his way when I went into the house to help you and got clobbered on the noggin."

"You shouldn't have come in," Ruth criticized.

Maggie wanted to say *Really?* but she held it in, knowing that Ruth had probably had a much worse day than she had.

She heard Ruth shift and it occurred to her that the poor woman's hands and feet were still tied.

"Here let me help," Maggie said. Again, she felt her way around in the dark until she found the rope that was tied around Ruth's legs. It was tight and her fingers ached as she tried to pry the knots apart.

"I don't understand why Mary Lou would do this," Maggie said. "She said you were—"

"Crazy?" Ruth guessed when Maggie stopped in mid-sentence.

"Well, yeah," Maggie admitted. She felt the rope give way and she swiftly unwound it from Ruth's skinny legs.

"I'm not," Ruth said.

It was clear from her sharp tone that she was irritated. Maggie couldn't really blame her. The crazy one, Mary Lou, had played them all, setting up Ruth to look like the nutter that she actually was.

"But why?" Maggie asked. "I don't understand."

"Because Mary Lou's father William Sutter is the illegitimate son of Jasper Kasey and Penelope Sutter," Ruth said.

Maggie gasped again.

"I know," Ruth said.

Maggie began to work on the knots around Ruth's wrists. "But Jasper was engaged to your mother."

Ruth sniffed. "Not for long. My mother got Jasper Kasey's number and broke off the engagement. Apparently she found out about his relationship with Penelope Sutter and that he had gotten her pregnant."

"But then he was with Ida Dixon," Maggie said.

"My mother tried to warn Ida that Jasper was a philanderer but Ida refused to listen. She was in love," Ruth said.

"How do you know all of this?" Maggie asked.

"I've been piecing it together since you discovered the skeleton," Ruth said. "Some of it was in my mother's diary and some of it came from other sources."

"Mary Lou gave me your mother's diary," Maggie said. "But there are pages missing."

Ruth let out a curse. "So that's what she's trying to do. She wants to make it look like my mother is the killer when it was really her grandmother."

Maggie untied the last knot and Ruth shook her hands out and rubbed her wrists.

"How do you know Penelope killed Jasper Kasey?" Maggie asked.

"Because it's the only thing that makes sense," Ruth said. "The Kasey family was from Dumontville and they were loaded. The Sutters were poor. Marrying Jasper would have changed Penelope's whole life. How could she not be angry that she was pregnant and he ditched her for Ida? Penelope must have killed Jasper in a rage and then buried him in the Dixon root cellar as the ultimate revenge."

"But why is Mary Lou trying to cover it up now?" Maggie asked. "It's not like she's going to jail for a crime her grandmother committed."

"Family honor," Ruth said. "It makes people do crazy things."

"What do you think she plans to do with us?" Maggie asked.

"At a guess?" Ruth asked. "Kill us."

The words hit Maggie in the chest with the weight and force of a boxer's gloved fist. Oh hell no.

"That's not happening," Maggie said.

She rose up on her knees and began to feel for a

doorknob. When she found it, she turned the handle only to discover it was locked, naturally.

"Be quiet," Ruth hissed. "If she hears you, she'll come for us."

"We're all the way in the backyard, she won't hear us. And even if she does, good," Maggie said. "I'm in the mood to kick her behind."

Her headache was easing, probably because rage and terror were pushing it out of her skull.

"Well, if you're going to be so pigheaded, let me help," Ruth said. "But be ready in case she's waiting for us."

Ruth muscled Maggie over and began to work on the lock. Maggie knelt down on the floor and tried to peak under the door. She got an eyeful of grass for her trouble and not much else. The light outside the door was weak, as if coming from a distance, probably the house.

She heard Ruth huff a breath and then she heard a click and the door swung open.

"Ha!" Ruth said. In the dim light, Maggie saw her shove a hairpin back into her hair. Impressive.

Ruth pushed up to a standing position and Maggie followed her. Her knees ached from being bent and her back felt bruised but she was ecstatic to be out of the shed and in the sweet fresh air.

"We have to get to the house," Maggie whispered.

Ruth bobbed her little birdlike head. She gestured for Maggie to follow her. Instead of going straight across the yard, they crept along the side, clinging to the cover of the shadows and the trees.

Even in the dark, Maggie could see that Ruth looked

pasty and weak. Maggie thought the poor woman needed a sandwich before she keeled over. Ruth had other ideas. She scurried around a large copse of trees and headed for the side of the house where she began to creep toward the front of the house.

"Where are you going?" Maggie asked. She rushed after her.

"To the front of the house," Ruth said.

"Why?" Maggie asked.

"Because if Sam came looking for you, who do you think is going to be Mary Lou's next victim?" Ruth asked. "If she hasn't gotten him already."

Maggie felt her heart plummet down to her feet. Ruth was right. Sam was the only other one who knew as much about the house as Ruth and Maggie. If Mary Lou was bent on keeping family secrets, she'd be going after Sam, too.

Chapter 28

It took just a couple minutes of stealth to get to the front yard. Maggie figured terror could do that for you.

"What do we do now?" Ruth asked.

"Find Sam," Maggie said.

"No duh," Ruth said. It was so singularly uncharacteristic of the older woman that it startled a half laugh out of Maggie.

"All right," she said. She peered into the front window, hoping to get a glimpse of what was happening. Her chest clutched a bit when she saw Sam's car parked in the driveway but no sign of Sam.

Ruth was behind her and nudged her with a pointy elbow to the back to get her in motion.

"Panic will not help him," Ruth whispered.

Maggie knew she was right. But when she saw that the front door of the house was open and no lights were on, her worst fears were realized. What if Mary Lou had killed Sam? Maggie didn't think she could bear it.

She stepped from behind the tree, planning to run into the house and call Sam's name. Ruth grabbed her by the back belt loop of her jeans and forcibly held her back. For such a little thing, Ruth had quite a grip.

"Let go!" Maggie demanded.

"No," Ruth snapped. "Get yourself together. Mary Lou can't know we've escaped or she's liable to go ballistic and then who knows what she'll do. You could be putting Sam at risk if you go flying in there."

Maggie blew out a breath. She knew Ruth was right, but still she wanted to run in and make sure Sam was okay.

"What do you suggest we do then?" she asked.

"Let's haunt her out," Ruth said. Even in the darkness, Maggie could see her white teeth gleam in a mischievous smile. "She's probably been the one who's been doing all of the haunting. Well, let's scare her silly."

"I like the way you think, Ruth," Maggie said. "Okay, we'll go in the back door and then we can split up inside and cover more ground that way."

Together they hurried back around the house. Maggie took the spare key that she had hidden under a flower pot on the back porch and carefully unlocked the door and let them in the house.

It was dark, and Maggie paused to listen. If Sam and Mary Lou were in here, she heard no sound to verify it, but Sam's car was still here so it stood to reason that if

Mary Lou had grabbed him, she had him in the house somewhere.

"I'll go upstairs," Ruth said. "You wait and see if she appears. My guess is she caught him in the basement since that's where she got me."

"What were you doing in my basement?" Maggie asked.

"Looking for my mother's diary," Ruth said. "Mary Lou set me up. She told me you had taken it."

"Me?"

Ruth gave her a sheepish look. "Sorry. I should have known better."

Maggie shrugged. "She tried to run me down with your car and I thought it was you."

"Me?" Ruth looked affronted.

"I'd say we're square," Maggie said. "Now let's not let her get us again. Be careful."

Ruth nodded. They crept through the kitchen and into the dining room. On a fold-out table in the corner, there was a stack of linens. Maggie felt her lips curve up. The mothers worked fast. She led the way into the main room where she and Sam had camped out in front of the fireplace.

The door to the cellar was open and the light from below cast a wide yellow rectangle across the floor. It took everything Maggie had not to run down the stairs and see if Sam was there.

"Wait for my signal," Ruth said and she squeezed Maggie's hand.

"What will it be?"

"Oh, you'll know it," Ruth said and she turned and hurried up the stairs.

Maggie retreated to the shadows, hoping that she and Ruth were doing the right thing. In moments, she heard a door creak and then slam. Even though she had expected it, it still made her jump.

She waited to see if Mary Lou would take the bait. She heard a voice from downstairs but no sound of movement.

Come on, Ruth, she thought. The lights flickered in the basement. Maggie had no idea how Ruth had managed that but she couldn't help but think, *Nice!*

The clatter of feet running down the hallway upstairs sounded and then two more doors slammed. This time there was movement in the basement, and Maggie pressed back into the shadows when Mary Lou came racing out of the basement door.

"Who's there?" she cried.

The light flicked on overhead, but it went right back out. Again, Maggie had no idea how Ruth was accomplishing these electrical feats, but she was awesome.

"Stop it!" Mary Lou cried. "I don't believe in you, Ida Dixon. You're dead. You can't hurt me."

A moan sounded from upstairs along with the creak of footsteps on the stairs.

"Who's there?" Mary Lou called again. She sounded frightened.

Maggie knew her chance to slip past Mary Lou and check the basement for Sam was fast approaching. If Ruth could just draw Mary Lou out a little bit more.

A door banged again and this time Mary Lou jumped. She tiptoed across the floor, glancing wildly around the room as if expecting a specter to jump out at her. But no, it was just Maggie slipping behind her to go down the basement steps.

When she got downstairs, she scanned the area. There was no sign of Sam. Had Mary Lou knocked him out and dragged him off somewhere like she had Ruth and Maggie? But then, why was Sam's car still here and what had Mary Lou been doing in the basement?

She heard several doors bang upstairs. Mary Lou yelled something and then the sound of running footsteps could be heard. Maggie figured Mary Lou was chasing Ruth through the house. She had to hurry before Mary Lou caught her. Ruth was spry but there was no way she could hold her own against the larger and younger Mary Lou.

Maggie walked the perimeter of the basement, hoping that Sam was just in a dark corner somewhere, but no. There was no sign of him. Beginning to feel frantic, Maggie hurried to the stairs. She was going to take Mary Lou out at the knees if she had to and demand to know where Sam was.

As she passed by the old root cellar where Jasper had been found, Maggie saw a set of parallel tracks in the dirt. It looked as if someone had been dragged into the old root cellar.

Maggie raced to the door and forced it open. Enough light shone in from the basement that she could see a body. Sick with dread, she dove at the familiar form of her fiancé.

He was lying on his side with his hands and feet bound and a piece of duct tape over his mouth. Maggie ripped off the tape and cupped his face in her hands.

"Mary Lou!" they said together.

Maggie kissed him quick and then set to work on his bound hands. The knots weren't as tight as the ones on Ruth, and Maggie made fast work of them.

"Where were you? How did you find me? Where's Ruth?" Sam asked.

"Ruth is upstairs trying to scare Mary Lou so I could get to you," Maggie said. "She had us tied up in the shed."

"But why?" Sam asked. "What does Mary Lou Sutter have to do with any of this?"

"Her father William Sutter is the illegitimate son of Penelope Sutter and Jasper Kasey," Maggie said.

Together they untied his legs and Sam rolled to his feet, stooping on his way out of the low-ceilinged room.

He took Maggie's hand in his and led the way out of the basement and up the stairs.

"We have to hurry," Maggie said. "If Mary Lou catches Ruth there is no telling what she'll do."

"Stay with me," Sam said.

"I promise," Maggie agreed. She really had no wish to take on the crazy woman all by herself.

At the top of the stairs, they paused to listen. Maggie found the lack of noise in the house more disturbing than the flickering lights, footsteps and door slams. At least when that was happening she had an idea of where everyone was.

"Ruth went upstairs," Maggie whispered.

Sam nodded and led the way out of the basement. They crept across the main room, through the dining room. Maggie paused to snatch one of the table linens off of the neatly folded pile. If nothing else, she figured she could hide under it if everything got too real.

They crept through the kitchen to a small door Maggie didn't remember.

"What's—," she began but Sam shushed her.

He opened the door which creaked a little, causing them both to freeze. When no other sounds were heard he continued to open the door. He pulled a chain and an overhead light snapped on.

Maggie looked over his shoulder at a narrow staircase. Then she looked at him.

"I found it when we were examining Jasper Kasey's remains," he said. "It's a back staircase that leads up to the master bedroom."

"Handy," Maggie said. "It's sure going to make those midnight ice cream binges easier."

Sam flashed a smile at her and led the way upstairs. Maggie noticed that he was stepping to the side of the stairs, probably to keep from stepping on the creaky middle. She did the same and they made it to the top without alerting anyone. Sam switched on the light and then slowly opened the door.

Thankfully it didn't creak, and it opened into the walk-in closet of the master bedroom. They stepped inside the closet but did not switch on the light. Maggie quietly shut the door to the stairs behind them.

Sam held on to Maggie's hand as he moved across the closet to the door. It was closed and he waited in front of it, listening. Maggie strained her ears trying to pick up noises but there was nothing.

Her heart hammered in her chest. She was worried about Ruth. If Mary Lou had been planning on killing them, there was really nothing stopping her now, and Maggie didn't think Ruth had the strength to fight for her life.

"Stay here," Sam said.

"What? No," Maggie protested.

"Just for a second," Sam insisted. "You'll be safe here."

"If this were a horror movie and you left me, one of us would die," Maggie argued.

"It's not a horror movie," Sam said. He squeezed her hand. "Just stay in the closet until I call for you. If you see or hear anything, call me and I'll come running."

Maggie was not happy about this. Mary Lou had already gotten the drop on each of them. Who knew if she already had Ruth? And now Sam wanted to go rogue and take on the crazy person by himself. She knew by the stubborn set to his jaw that he wasn't going to have it any other way.

"Fine but be careful," she said.

She watched as he slipped through the door with a sick feeling of dread in her gut. She officially hated everything about this.

Maggie kept the door open a crack. Not that she could see anything more than shadows, but still she felt better trying to monitor the situation. Of course, just like every game of hide-and-seek she'd ever played, now she had to go to the bathroom.

She bounced on her feet, trying to take her mind off her need for the facility. She couldn't see Sam. She didn't hear any noise at all in the house and the lights stayed off, adding to the creepy quotient.

She bounced and jiggled her leg and paced a little bit but the silence and the darkness seemed never-ending. Finally, she couldn't take it anymore. She slipped out of the closet and stood in the bedroom.

It was then that she saw Ruth come through the doorway, heading straight for her.

Chapter 29

"Ruth!" she cried with relief. "Where have you been? Are you all right? Where's Mary Lou?"

"Right here," Mary Lou said as she stomped into the room.

Maggie could only make out her bulky shape in the darkness but it was enough.

"The closet!" she cried at Ruth. Maggie yanked the door open and she and Ruth hurried inside. Maggie slammed the door behind them and dashed across the small space to the other door. "Come on, down here!"

Maggie bolted down the stairs, leading Ruth to the kitchen. Once they were through, she slammed the door behind them, hoping it took Mary Lou a minute to figure out there was a door in the closet and that they had just escaped through it.

"We need to find Sam," Maggie said. "Come on."

She hurried through the kitchen, tossing the table-cloth she still held onto her shoulder.

"Sam!" Maggie cried. "Sam!"

Footsteps pounded down the main staircase and Sam appeared at the bottom.

"Mary Lou found us in the bedroom," Maggie gasped. "I think she's going to try to come through the kitchen."

"Got it," Sam said. "Stay here, both of you."

Maggie was about to protest when an enraged battle cry sounded from the dining room. There was no mistaking that it was Mary Lou and that she was unhappy.

Sam moved in front of Maggie and Ruth but Mary Lou didn't even slow down. She took him out like a wrecking ball with a head butt to the middle.

"Sam!" Maggie cried. She had no time to help, however, as Mary Lou reared up and glared at her and Ruth.

"You ruined everything!" she cried. "My whole life would have been different if it hadn't been for you."

Maggie turned to look at Ruth, who was sadly shaking her head at Mary Lou.

"If Jasper had just married my grandmother, we would have been raised with the Kasey fortune, but no, he left her and my daddy for you!"

Maggie narrowed her eyes at Ruth. She looked paler than usual and her hair was different. Maggie felt her own hair begin to rise on the back of her neck.

"That's why my grandmother killed him, because he was going to leave her for you. He was buried in your house and you never even knew it!" Mary Lou tipped her head back and let out a deranged laugh.

Maggie felt Sam rise up next to her, snatch the table-cloth from her shoulder and toss it over Mary Lou's head.

"Ah!" Mary Lou screamed and she started to kick and punch.

Sam subdued her with a bear hug.

"Maggie, in my pocket are some plastic zip tie cuffs, grab them for me, would you?"

Maggie was still staring at Ruth with her mouth agape.

Mary Lou started to buck.

"Maggie, help!" Sam cried.

"Oh, right, sorry," Maggie said. She jumped into motion, finding the ties in his pants pocket and then wrestling with Mary Lou to get her wrists together so Sam could let go of her to get the restraints on.

Mary Lou let out a shriek of rage and Maggie whipped the cloth off her head.

"It's over," Maggie snapped. "Knock it off."

Mary Lou collapsed to the floor and began to weep. Knowing that she had planned to kill them all, Maggie could not find it in herself to feel sorry for the woman.

As Mary Lou curled up into a ball, sniffling and whining, Maggie threw her arms around Sam and hugged him tight. He was okay. That was all that mattered. Sam squeezed her in return and she felt him plant a kiss in her hair.

"This was by far the most terrifying evening of my life," he said. He leaned back to look at her. "You're okay, really okay?"

"I'm fine," Maggie said. "And you?"

"Never better," he said. He wrapped his arms around her again. "When I got here, I ran right down to the basement, thinking that's where you'd be. I was so scared when your phone went dead that I forgot twenty years of police training and walked right into an ambush. Crazy eyes there clobbered me."

"Me, too," Maggie said. "You were right. I never should have entered the house, but if something had happened to Ruth while I stood outside . . ."

"And that is the dilemma with police work," Sam said. "You're always trying to out think the bad guys."

Maggie glanced behind her. Her accomplice was moving across the floor toward the stairs.

"Ruth . . . ?" Maggie began but then her voice trailed off. This time she could see the woman more clearly and it wasn't Ruth. "Ida?"

She glanced up at Sam and saw him staring in wide-eyed wonder at the same apparition. Mary Lou wept on, oblivious.

The woman took on a bit more substance than she'd had before and Maggie could see that she wore old-fashioned clothes, like something out of the forties.

She waved to them and mouthed the words, "Be happy here."

Then she turned and went up the stairs, slowly fading away before she reached the top.

Maggie and Sam were both staring at the spot where she had vanished when Ruth appeared at the top of the stairs. "What are you two staring at?"

Maggie looked at Sam and he looked at her. They both looked back at Ruth and said, "Nothing."

Ruth glanced down at their feet at Mary Lou.

"Hot dog! You got her," Ruth said. "Would it be police brutality if *I* kicked her in the pants?"

"No, but you still aren't allowed to," Sam said.

"Even if you turn your back for just a second, and I just happen to trip?" Ruth persisted.

"I'm not turning my back," Sam said. "In fact, I'm going to take her outside to await her ride to the hospital."

"Fine," Ruth said. She kicked at the floor and Maggie wasn't sure but she thought she heard Ruth call Sam a party pooper.

They watched as Sam pulled Mary Lou up by the elbow and led her out the door to await medical attention.

"Are you all right?" Maggie asked Ruth.

Ruth held up a sheaf of papers. "I am now."

"You found the missing diary pages?" Maggie asked.

"They were in the upstairs sitting room, on the window seat next to your wedding gown, which is going to get all wrinkly by the way, you should really hang it up," Ruth said.

"Wedding gown?" Maggie asked.

"Yes, your gown," Ruth said. Then she made a face. "Oh, do not tell me that Mary Lou stole that from you."

"Show me," Maggie said.

"All right," Ruth said. She gave Maggie a funny look

and led the way up the stairs and down the hall to the sitting room.

Maggie flipped on all of the lights as they went and was pleased to see that they stayed on.

"So, how did you manage to flicker the basement lights from up here?" Maggie asked.

Ruth gave her an abashed look. "About that . . . I was so busy reading the diary pages, I sort of forgot to pretend to be the ghost."

Maggie looked at her. "So, you didn't do the door slamming and flickering lights and footsteps running up and down the halls?"

"It sounded like you had it under control," Ruth said. She shrugged. "Too much would have been overkill."

They entered the empty sitting room and Maggie stopped short. Draped across the window seat was a beautiful blue silk dress with a white lace overlay. She picked it up and it rustled like leaves in the wind in her fingers. She held it up to her front and glanced at her reflection in the window. It looked to be a perfect fit.

Ruth stepped up behind Maggie and studied her reflection as well. "You're going to be a beautiful bride," she said. "Sam Collins is a lucky man."

Maggie was pretty sure it was the only compliment Ruth had ever paid her, which made it mean that much more.

"Thank you," she said. "I think I'll take the dress and have it pressed and cleaned for the wedding."

She paused to listen for any footsteps or door slams or any signs of spectral protest. There was nothing.

As Maggie walked down the stairs with her wedding

dress over her arm, she tried to tell herself that it was not possible that Ida Dixon had manifested a dress for her, but a tiny little part of her hoped that somehow she had. It just seemed right to start her new life in her new home with something of Ida's, and how perfect that it was something old, borrowed and blue all rolled into one?

They stepped outside just as the ambulance was pulling out of the driveway. Sam stood on the porch steps waiting for them and Maggie felt the need to hug him tight just one more time.

Today could have gone so differently, but they'd gotten lucky. She couldn't help but think that Ida Dixon had been hanging around just waiting for someone to put the events of the past to rights.

Maggie was glad that she and Sam had been able to do it. She figured the dress was Ida's way of giving them her blessing. She was humbled by it.

"Are you all right?" Sam asked.

"Never better," Maggie said.

Sam leaned down and kissed her and Maggie heard Ruth make a choking sound.

"Eh, save it for the honeymoon," she said. She stomped off the porch and over to the police car.

Sam and Maggie followed, trying to hide their laughter.

Chapter 30

"Aw, Mom, you look amazing," Laura Gerber said. She adjusted the pearl hair clip that held Maggie's hair in place in her half-up, half-down hairdo and stood back to study it.

Maggie was seated at the Louis XVI–style vanity, which had once belonged to Ida Dixon and was a wedding present from Sam, in the master bedroom of her new home. Downstairs she could hear the commotion of the guests as they arrived and made their way through the house to the backyard where the festivities were to be held.

"Thanks, honey," Maggie said. "I'm so tickled that you're standing up for me. It means so much to me and Sam."

"Are you kidding?" Laura asked. She twirled and her sea foam–green dress swirled around her knees. "I get a new dress and I get to see my mom marry the love of her life. I wouldn't miss it."

"Your dad—" Maggie began but Laura cut her off.

"Would absolutely approve," Laura said. She rested her hands on her mother's shoulders and their gazes met in the mirror's reflection. They were wearing matching strands of pearls at their throats that Charlie had bought for them shortly after Laura was born. "Dad was the love of your life once upon a time, and he'll always be in your heart, but Sam is the love of your life right now, and I couldn't be happier for both of you."

Maggie's throat felt suspiciously tight. She swallowed and it eased just a little. "I love you, honey."

"I love you, too, Mom," Laura said.

There was a knock on the door and they both called, "Come in."

Maggie's mother, sister and all of the Good Buy Girls hurried into the room. They were ready for a party in sparkly, bright-hued dresses, snappy shoes and festive jewelry. To Maggie, they looked like a flock of exotic birds, who brightened up the nearly empty room with their plumage.

It was late afternoon, and Michael Claramotta had been working his smokers since the day before and the whole neighborhood was flavored with the scent of barbecue with a hint of bacon since, once he'd heard about Dot's recommendation for a bacon station, he'd been all in.

"We just wanted to check and make sure you have everything you need," Ginger said. She looked a little watery around the eyeballs and Maggie noted that she had a tissue wadded up in her fist.

"I do," Maggie said.

"Now save that for later," Joanne teased and they all laughed. It was the breathless, excited, nervous laugh that preceded a life-changing event.

Maggie nodded. Looking at her nearest and dearest made her feel weepy again, in the best possible way, and she wasn't sure she could speak without blubbering.

"You look red eyed," Summer said. "You haven't been drinking, have you? Because that never goes well."

"No!" Maggie protested and then laughed, which she suspected was what Summer had been going for.

"You look beautiful, baby," Lizzie said.

"Thanks, Mom," Maggie said.

"A real knock-out," Sissy agreed. She put a clear vase with a big bouquet of peonies and calla lilies in it on the vanity. "Your bouquet."

Maggie looked at her in question and Sissy smiled. "Sam had the florist add the calla lilies. He said you'd understand."

Maggie nodded. It was just one more reason why she had lost her heart to that man.

There was a discreet knock on the door, and then Blue Dixon stuck his head around the door frame.

"Sorry to interrupt, but Pastor Shields has asked that the ladies be escorted to their seats as the groom is getting a might antsy down there."

Maggie rose from her seat and looked through the sheer curtain at the backyard. Sure enough, it was standing room only in the yard and Sam was pacing by the large white garden arch that was swathed in tulle and peonies.

She could see the Good Buy Girls' significant others were standing with him, talking and joking as they each stole glances at the back of the house to see where their ladies were.

She was going to marry Sam! The thought filled her up from the inside out and it was all she could do to keep herself from running out the door and down the stairs to get to him.

"Well, you heard him," Summer said. She started to shoo everyone out of the room. "We do not want a groom on the run. Let's go!"

They each hugged Maggie on their way out, wishing her luck and dabbing at their eyes as the tears of joy began to flow.

Blue Dixon had escorted Lizzie to the wedding, and Maggie found there was something right about that as well. As he waited for Lizzie to stop fussing with Laura's hair, he stood beside Maggie and looked at her with approval.

"Ida's dress looks lovely on you, my dear," he said.

Maggie's eyes went wide. "Ida's? How did you know?"

He looked embarrassed and then said, "When I gave you the items from storage, something made me hold that dress aside. Then one night, I dreamt that Ida demanded that I get up in the middle of the night and deliver the dress to this house. The next day when I woke I thought it was the strangest dream ever, but when I went to my closet to see where the dress had been hanging, it was gone."

They exchanged wide-eyed looks and Maggie said, "She wanted me to have it."

"Yes, I believe she did," he said. "And she was right. You are absolutely breathtaking."

"Thank you, Blue," Maggie said.

He bowed his head and turned to escort Lizzie from the room. Her mother gave her a tiny finger wave and headed out the door on Blue's arm.

"Are you ready, Mom?" Laura asked.

Maggie paused to listen to the house. There were no cold spots, no flickering lights, no slamming doors, nothing. There was a sense of contentment in the old place that eased Maggie into a feeling of deep and abiding peace.

She turned and grinned at her daughter. "Yes, I am."

The ceremony was simple. The vows were traditional. The Good Buy Girls wept, along with a good many other attendees, with the joy that weddings bring. But laughter won out when Maggie's grandnephew Josh felt compelled to stand on his chair and shout in his bossy three-year-old voice, "Kiss her, Uncle Sam!"

Sam did. The band played. Everyone danced, but the makeshift floor was owned by Doc Franklin and his wife, Alice. Ginger's cake received rave reviews and Michael's barbecue was a hit but not quite as big of a hit as the bacon station, which Dot and her boyfriend, Javier, circled repeatedly.

When the night started to wind down, Sam and Maggie

slipped away from their guests and hid in the lilac bushes that lined the yard.

"Well, you've been Mrs. Sam Collins for five hours now," Sam said. He pulled her into his arms so they were facing each other. "How does it feel?"

"Honestly?" Maggie asked. She looped her arms around his neck to pull him even closer. "Never better. I think I scored the bargain of my life when I married you."

Sam laughed and hugged her hard. "How do you figure?"

"Well, I now have a wonderful man to share my bed, pay half the bills, start a new life in a new-to-me house, and he's the sheriff so we can investigate crimes together. All this at the rock-bottom price of saying 'I do.' Seriously, it's a smokin' good deal."

Sam kissed her. It was a knee-buckler, and Maggie had to hold on tight so that she didn't wilt into a puddle right then and there. When he pulled back, he pressed his forehead to hers.

"I'm glad you think so," he said. "Because this bargain is an all-sales-final sort of situation."

Maggie laughed. "I wouldn't have it any other way."

The sheriff and the bargain hunter lived happily ever after, and usually, at 50% off.

The Good Buy Girls' Wedding Bargain Tips

1. Being the queen of thrift and resale, Maggie recommends looking there first for your wedding dress. Many designer dresses with original prices of three to five thousand dollars wind up in secondhand stores where they're sold for a fraction of the original price. The key to finding the perfect secondhand dress is to give yourself plenty of time to search in stores and online.

2. Ginger is all about the cake, wedding cake that is. To save on the cost of the cake, she recommends ordering a smaller two-tier custom cake to be put on display while using a back-up sheet cake of the same flavor to be served to the guests.

3. Wedding favors are Summer's forte. She believes the best wedding favor is a consumable like Tyler's honey that can do double duty as a treat for the guest but also serve to mark the special day. Some of her favorites include personalized cookies or candies, which are cheaper when bought in bulk.

4. Claire believes that the entertainment portion of the wedding is the most important as that is what the guests tend to remember the most. To save money on music, look for a smaller band or go with just a DJ to spin your favorite music. Another way to save money is to have the ceremony and the reception at the same location and have the band or DJ provide the music for both.

5. Joanne steered Maggie in the right direction for the food. Offering comfort food, like barbecue, and letting guests serve themselves at strategically located food stations will cut the cost and is a lot more fun than a swanky seven course meal.

6. Sam and Maggie nailed it by using their own house to host the wedding and reception. Using one location for both the wedding and reception always saves money but using their own house made it even more cost effective and renting larger tables means less centerpieces!

The delicious mysteries of Berkley Prime Crime for gourmet detectives

Julie Hyzy
WHITE HOUSE CHEF MYSTERIES

B. B. Haywood
CANDY HOLLIDAY MURDER MYSTERIES

Jenn McKinlay
CUPCAKE BAKERY MYSTERIES

Laura Childs
TEA SHOP MYSTERIES

Claudia Bishop
HEMLOCK FALLS MYSTERIES

Nancy Fairbanks
CULINARY MYSTERIES

Cleo Coyle
COFFEEHOUSE MYSTERIES

Solving crime can be a treat.

penguin.com